HOOP'S TRUTH
A Novella

Gloria Lynn Howe

ARCHWAY
PUBLISHING

Archway Publishing books may be ordered through booksellers or by contacting:

Archway Publishing
1663 Liberty Drive
Bloomington, IN 47403
www.archwaypublishing.com
1 (888) 242-5904

Because of the dynamic nature of the Internet, any web addresses or links contained in this book may have changed since publication and may no longer be valid. The views expressed in this work are solely those of the author and do not necessarily reflect the views of the publisher, and the publisher hereby disclaims any responsibility for them.

Any people depicted in stock imagery provided by Getty Images are models, and such images are being used for illustrative purposes only. Certain stock imagery © Getty Images.

Scripture taken from the American Standard Version of the Bible. Public Domain

ISBN: 978-1-4808-8551-6 (sc)
ISBN: 978-1-4808-8552-3 (e)

Library of Congress Control Number: 2019919639

Print information available on the last page.

Archway Publishing rev. date: 01/07/2020

"Hoop's Truth"- A Novella

By: Gloria Lynn Howe

"Hoop's Truth"– A Novella is an enjoyable and quick read! It provides you with a short look into the lives of the realistic characters that make up Hoop's family.

Told in snap-shots, it reminded me of what it was like to "stay in a child's place" growing up, knowing just enough to not really know anything. Although you see portions of each person, every character is relatable and you find yourself truly connecting to them.

This story mixes basketball, with family, and even gives you a small glimpse of sorority life. I had such fun reading this book from Hoop's perspective. It really gives you a sense of the organized chaos in the Hoop's understanding- quietly observing, yet remaining true to her focus, passion and family.

Ameerah Holliday,
Ebb & Flow Publications

Foreword

Listen, we all know these people! We have gone to school with them. We have married them. We have hung out with them and we have loved them at times.

Ms. Howe has written a CAN NOT put down book! You want to know what is going to happen to these people. Will Abeba's sexual addition come under control? Will she become a major star? The only way that you will find out is to read the book!

Ms. Howe certainly has a treasure chest full of characters in her brain. And they all come alive on these remarkable pages. It's a wonderful reading and a great escape!!!!!!

Actress, BeBe Drake

Dedication

I am most proud to dedicate this book to a person with whom I've had a connection with my entire life. God truly made no mistakes. Your belief matched with my implacable questioning, lead us directly to one another. Now I have a reason to "sign" you **Calvin C. Taylor**, my Dad.

Here's to the next chapter of our lives shared together. I am thankful that our families have grown. I look forward to creating memories with you, my sister and brother.

In memoriam:

I also dedicate this book to my mother **Patricia Howe**, a beautiful, generous, charismatic and strong woman. I see you each time I look at myself in the mirror. Our smiles are identical. I am proud to have been your one and only.

As a toddler, I heard and understood everything that was uttered from your muted voice. We had our own communication.

Through instincts, gestures and some sign language, I understood. Through those years of separation until your final day with cancer- I still understood. The battle was not yours-it was the Lord's.

Thank you for giving me life. Although your life was short; it was not in vain. I am your living proof. As you watch me from heaven above, I hope that I've made you proud. I will always love you.

Your one and only daughter,
Gloria

*To **Shirley Chambers**, the mother who raised me as her own. It was God's will to bring you home when he did. Your job had been done. Throughout my childhood you protected and prepared me to survive in a world that may not always accept me based on my race or gender.*

You encouraged me to keep God in my life and to trust in his word. You also insisted that I receive a quality education, attend college, be civically aware and involved, develop a good work ethic and to respect diverse cultures. You were a humble woman, yet confident; a firm woman, yet fair.

You challenged me to see the world. As I traveled to some countries without you, I knew your spirit was with me. Thank you for what you've deposited into my spirit. Thank you for teaching me how to live. I love and miss you dearly.

Your daughter,
Gloria

WNBA Dedication

We all have it, that cadenced pound that beats steadily like a rebounded ball against a 94 by 50 feet basketball court. It's that rigor that leads us up and down the court of life. That beat, that guiding force that pushes our inner selves to persevere and overcome obstacles through life's unexpected everything. That it is called determination

It is my honor to make a special WNBA dedication to a woman who has pushed through and overcome personal and career challenges with grace. Her illustrious basketball coaching career began on the historic grounds of **Cheyney State College, the nation's oldest HBCU founded in 1837.**

In 1982, the NCAA recognized the Lady Wolves Women's Basketball Team for their talent and rigor. That 28th day of March also marked the day that the world recognized the *spirited coach* who encouraged them. The world watched as they challenged the top ranked Louisiana Tech during a CBS broadcast of the Division 1 intercollegiate women's basketball tournament. The petite, powerhouse woman who led the Lady Wolves, later became a champion in her own right.

In 2001, she was inducted into the Women's Basketball Hall of Fame while serving as an assistant coach for the gold-medal winning 2004 U.S. Olympic Team. In 2018, her accomplishments lead her to become the first African American female to reach her record of 1,000[th] wins as the Head Coach of The Rutgers

University Scarlet Knights Women's Basketball Team- **Mrs. C. Vivian Stringer**.

In 1983 Cheyney was renamed as Cheyney University of Pennsylvania.

My Truth

As an educator, I vowed to educate, protect and inspire generations of elementary to secondary grade level students. I've learned through students and many have touched my life in special ways. I still remember some of their faces, personalities and voices; particularly the louds ones. My experiences from teaching in the South Bronx to Mount Vernon, New York were immeasurable. I taught almost everything from biology, chemistry, theater arts, dance, common core English language arts to summer-school and homebound studies. I was driven.

One afternoon I attended an urgent meeting at school. During that meeting, a new student was discussed. It seemed like the entire cavalry of the school's administrative staff was present along with a few other teachers. I was given a thin book to read that was filled with illustrations. I was asked to take it home and to do some research before meeting the student and parents the following day. My takeaway from the meeting was that I would receive a student with special needs and perhaps that student would be accompanied by a para–professional teaching assistant. I was correct.

I reported to school the next morning and taught my AP English class as normal. I later learned that teaching as normal was exactly what I needed to do. There were times that I did not believe my lesson adaptations and or accommodations were sufficient.

However, as the year went on, the student and I seemed to develop a rhythm. We learned together. Yes, there were odd moments; but we got through them. It warmed my heart each time the student insisted on expressing what they'd learned in class;

even if it was well into their lunch period. At the end of the year, my supervisor expressed to me that I was entrusted to assist the student and family. I will always remember that student and what they taught me. It is one of my most memorable and gratifying teaching experiences.

"Make your teachers understand that they have to teach the way you learn," **Anthony Ianni, Former Michigan State Center, who has overcome Autism challenges and bullying.**

Hoop's Truth

My name is Hooper Ellen Hill, but everyone calls me Hoop. When I was younger, I was on the fast track to becoming a female basketball star! I played on the junior varsity and varsity teams in both middle and high school. Coaches from all the major colleges came to see me play. *Truth is…so did the coaches from the WNBA and the NBA. That was… until the change.*

The night of my last game I scored 28 points and 12 rebounds. That's all I remember.

The doctors diagnosed me as having Asperger Syndrome. It's a developmental disorder that affects the ability to effectively socialize and communicate. The disorder, also known as Autism Spectrum Disorder, ASD, is on the high functioning end of the autism spectrum. It can last for years or for a lifetime.

Mama and Mr. James said they noticed the **dIFfeREnCe** in me when I was 10. At times I say inappropriate things and curse. Sometimes people think I also have the "Tourette Syndrome" tic; but **truth is**… I've been *cursing* for years. Who am I? I am a 6'5" athlete. I love boys and basketball trivia. Does that sound so special to you?

Let me introduce you to some colorful characters- my family and their friends. They live everywhere from New York to Los Angeles. To them, I'm the one who's special; but after you see what's going on in their lives, you might see things from a different perspective. Each of their stories is presented in a unique vignette; giving you just enough to see *who's different, odd, unbalanced, depressed, strange, freaky, conceited, ratchet and wise.* Are you ready?

Autism & Basketball Matters!

Anthony Ianni was the first Division 1 college basketball player with autism. He played for **Michigan State University**. He is a dedicated supporter of **Coaches Powering Forward for Autism**.

"It was really tough growing up, but that's where basketball came into play…I know not everybody on the spectrum will have the same success as me; but what happened to me can be a goal of many parents who have kids on the spectrum. Autism doesn't define who you are. You define who you are," **Anthony Ianni**.

In 2019, **Kalin Bennett**, a **Kent State Golden Flashes Men's Basketball** recruit, became the first autistic individual to play a team sport at the NCAA Division 1 level. Bennett, who plays center for the Flashes, is listed at 6 feet, 11 inches tall and 300 pounds.

"It's good to know that people look up to me, but the real thing is: Everybody is capable of doing whatever they want to do in life. I hope I created a thing that's going to transcend to more kids so they believe in themselves first and foremost," **Kalin Bennett**.

The Utah Jazz, Cleveland Cavaliers, Sacramento Kings and the Oklahoma City Thunder NBA teams created sensory rooms designed for children with autism spectrum disorder and other intellectual and developmental disabilities at their home arenas.

Contents

1

Salon Drama

Unique Beauty Salon, New York, New York

Saturday morning 7:00 a.m., an exhausted Reesa, filled with shame and emotion, wiped a steady stream of tears from her face as she entered the office of her upscale East Manhattan hair salon. She stood in front of the new mirror, now perched firmly against the exposed brick wall. Hours earlier, she and Jeffrey, her top stylist and best friend, posed in front of it, as he styled her hair in preparation for her date.

She knew Jeffrey would be coming in soon; but she could not stop crying. At 7:15 a.m. the front door sensor alerted. It was Jeffrey. She tried to pull herself to together; but the redness surrounding her big brown eyes and the swelling were easily recognizable. She knew Jeffrey could sense a crisis or drama a mile away; but there was nowhere to hide.

"Whew! Hey, Boss Lady! It's **raining cats and dogs** out there. And you know rain and hair don't mix. If a few divas cancel today, can I pay my booth rent tomorrow? Ree! ... Ree! Ree! Do you hear me," a boisterous Jeffrey asked?

Reesa tried to avoid facing Jeffrey. She kept her back turned. Jeffrey noticed the avoidance immediately.

With his hands on his voluptuous hips, Jeffrey stared at Reesa then teasingly broached, "How bout we start with hello? As my mother used to say, **even a dog will wag its tail** if a person walked into a room," he snapped.

With her back still turned she mumbled, "Good morning Jeffrey."

"Well damn! How rude," Jeffrey admonished!

"Can't you see that I'm busy," Reesa shouted!

Reesa stormed off toward the front waiting area of the salon.

The two-floor salon is housed in a three-story brownstone. It's located on East 52nd Street between 5th and 6th Avenues in Manhattan. The salon is Reesa's home away from home. She lives in a quiet, suburban neighborhood in the Riverdale section of the Bronx.

She loves her neighborhood mainly because it borders the Henry Hudson River. It's a **stone's throw** from the city; an ideal locale for a singled entrepreneur like Reesa.

The majority of her time is spent at the salon. She designed it to fit her personal style. It's a decorative mixture of architecture, culture and personal items collected from her frequent trips to Africa and Europe.

However, today, not even the beautiful artwork and paintings that surround her, could shake her bewildered feelings. She wondered how she allowed herself to be deceived by a man she had responsibly dated for eight months. She cried out loud as glimpses of their past conversations played out in her head. She remembered how they discussed traveling and building a future together.

She grew angry and internalized her feelings. She blamed herself for being vulnerable. Why her she wondered? How could she have been played like a pawn in a psychological game of chess?

She aggressively rearranged pillows, throws, magazines and

anything she could get her hands on. Jeffrey dropped everything and ran to the waiting area to calm her down.

He grabbed her by the arm, and swung her tall, thin body around. "Reesa, who do you think you're fooling? **I wasn't born yesterday**! You were on **cloud 9** before I left last night. Talk to me," he demanded!

"Jeffrey, just leave it alone. I don't want to talk about it," Reesa shouted!

"Did he hurt you? Do I need to go over there and whup some ass," Jeffrey asked?

Reesa began to cry.

"This fool got my Ree Ree crying in her own establishment! What is his address? I'm going over there," Jeffrey demanded!

"No," Reesa shouted!

"Jeffrey lowered his voice and asked, "Do we need to call the police Ree," Jeffrey asked?

Reesa slowly raised her head and looked Jeffrey square in his eyes and said, "No, Jeffrey it wasn't anything like that; but let's just say, **I've made my bed and now I have to lie in it**."

"Do you want me to send a few homo thugs over there? I've got a few numbers locked in my phone," Jeffrey said.

"No Jeffrey! I don't want him assaulted! I don't want anything coming back to me and I definitely don't need any salon drama. This is my place of business," Reesa said.

Jeffrey, somewhat relieved, then said, "Well girl hurry up and **spill the tea**, before our clients get here."

The two nestled closely together on the tan chaise in the waiting area as Reesa filled Jeffrey in.

"It turned out that Mr., tall, fine and wealthy was living a double life," Reesa explained.

"Okay before you start, please tell me that the evening began at a five-star restaurant," he asked?

"Yes! I met him at the Carlyle," Reesa replied.

"#COINS! Carry on," Jeffrey said.

"He sent a car to the salon to get me," she explained.

"Wait, what? Why didn't he drive," Jeffrey asked?

"Can I get through the story? He told me he was leaving his car at his office. He asked if he could send a car for me so we wouldn't lose our reservation. I appreciated the gesture," Reesa said. She began to cry again.

"Why are you crying? No man is worth your tears! How he gonna leave his never-seen-before Bentley in a garage and send a driver for you? I wished you would have driven your Mercedes to the Carlyle. That way you could have left his ass as soon as the date started **going south**," Jeffrey declared!

"I should've known better. I didn't notice any red flags or maybe I didn't want to notice," Reesa cried loudly!

"No! We are not going there. You know that when you cry. I cry. I beat my face with Mac this morning and I am not trying to wipe it off. Diva, please pull it together. We've got customers coming in soon. Well tell me about what you ordered for dinner," Jeffrey asked?

Reesa obliged. "I ordered the Herb Crusted Salmon," Reesa said.

"Ooh. I heard the salmon was everything. Now **cut to the chase**," he demanded!

After Reesa gathered herself, she described intimate details about her spoiled overnight date.

"After dinner I was ready. I was really ready. I've been celibate for four years. I knew that last night was the perfect time for me to give myself to him with absolutely no regrets," Reesa said.

"Girl I hope you ain't about to tell me you that the two of you made a damn a sex tape. You know you can't do what white folks do! Harold told me that everything goes up into the clouds. Pictures and videos be floating all around and shit," Jeffrey rambled.

"No. We did not! And who the hell is Harold," Reesa asked?

"Harold is my new Boo-friend. I met him at the Apple Store. Now he's my personal Apple genius if you know what I mean? He's taking me out for drinks this Thursday," Jeffrey rambled.

"Jeffrey! Jeffrey! I don't care about your new geek freak of the week or your cracked phone," Reesa sharply said!

"Oh no she didn't! I was just looking out for you. At least I don't have to worry about my goodies bouncing from cloud to cloud and over rainbows," Jeffrey said.

"Please Jeffrey," Reesa pleaded!

"After dinner we caught a cab to the Westside," Reesa said with laugh.

"What's so funny," Jeffrey asked?

"Damn he was smooth. I told him long ago that I loved horses. He remembered me saying that after living in New York for almost 30 years, I'd never taken a romantic horse and carriage ride through Central Park. That's what we did. He showered me with champagne and roses. The night was magical," Reesa recalled.

"Wow, just like Brandy and them who played Cinderella," Jeffrey said.

"We took another cab to his condo on the Upper Westside. That's where we made passionate love all night. He made me quiver and shake in places that had never been touched or stimulated before. It was beautiful," Reesa said with her head tilted and eyes closed tight.

"Well damn! Your date sounded tasty! #theDwasgood," Jeffrey declared!

"Things went downhill this morning. While he showered the house phone rang. A name and number scrolled across the television screen. I didn't pay much attention to it until after the phone rang again. It was the same number. When he returned to the bedroom, I told him that he'd missed a call," Reesa said.

"Okay, well what did he say," Jeffrey asked?

"He said thanks," Reesa replied.

"Ooh, this is getting good," Jeffrey said as he hunkered down.

"When I entered the bathroom, I immediately spotted a gold wedding band on the countertop of the sink. It was right there! In my face next to his shaving bag," Reesa shouted!

Reesa suddenly burst into tears as she heard her voice repeat the events of last night.

"You didn't see a wedding band earlier? Not even a tan line around his finger," Jeffrey asked?

"No! Nothing! If I did, we wouldn't be having this goddamn conversation,"

Reesa shouted!

"Ump, ump, ump! He must be used to thots or thirsty and lonely women who settle. Anyone can clearly see that you do not fit into either one of those categories! #Ican'thonty," Jeffrey shouted!

"When I returned to the bedroom, he was in the other room on the phone.

I heard him say, "My conference ends today. I'll be home tonight." That confirmed it all. I didn't need to ask him not one, damn, thing," Reesa said slowly.

Jeffrey dropped to his knees and bowed his head. "Father God, you know I'm not a strong man; but please let her tell me this was when she went upside his head with a shoe, a purse or something," he prayed.

"No Jeffrey, I did not. I wouldn't have made it in business or in life without learning self-control. Besides, I'm a lady. **I strike when the iron's hot**," Reesa said.

"Yaaasss! You ain't never lied; so what happened after that Boss," Jeffery asked?

I walked into the living room. He was still on the phone, so I began to towel dry slowly. And I do mean slowly in every sense of the word. Then I loved on myself. I moisturized every inch of my smooth, voluptuous, caramel body," Reesa said.

"Werkk, Diva," Jeffrey exclaimed!

"He stood silently with the phone to his ear and a towel wrapped around his waist. He watched me like a hawk. He didn't know what to do; but I knew just what he wanted. He was stiff and erect, like a Buckingham Palace guard standing at full attention.

When I was done, he ended his call and followed me into the bedroom. He couldn't keep his hands off me. He begged for round… uh none of your business Jeffrey. That's when I told him that I had forgotten about an early appointment. I promised to make it up to him. Shortly after we got dressed," Reesa said.

"Is that it? Damn you are gangsta," Jeffrey shouted!

"Oh no. As we were saying our goodbyes at the door, I whispered softly in his ear. 'You might need this when you go home tonight baby.' He said 'I am home.' That's when I placed the wedding band in his hands and said, 'Thank you for making last night unforgettable. I absolutely love your condo; but I can bet that your wife in Westchester County or in Jersey doesn't have the key.' Then I closed the door behind me and caught a cab here," Reesa said.

"Damn, Reesa. I am so sorry you went through that. You did everything right. You stuck to your standards and you didn't rush into things with this man. I checked his background records, social media accounts, the dating sites and everything. I thought he was the one for sure. Has he tried to contact you," Jeffery asked?

"As a matter of fact, he has. He sent a long text saying that he was going through a nasty divorce. He still shares a home with his wife and children in New Jersey… yadda, yadda, yadda," Reesa said.

"Reesa, I have no doubt that you will meet someone who has already unpacked and thrown out his baggage," Jeffrey declared!

"How can someone lie about who they are so easily? Wait! I think I remember the name. Was it Deshawn? Delores or Diane," Reesa pondered.

"How about Debbie dumb ass," Jeffrey joked.

"Ha! I needed that. Debbie? Hmm. Debra Moore? That's it! Her name was Debra Moore," Reesa shouted!

"Bless her heart whatever the name. Let me get ready for my first customer. She travels in from New Jersey and will be **fit to be tied** if she's not in and out of this salon in time to beat the traffic over the George Washington Bridge.

Wayment!!!!! Chil... I need to sit down. Say it ain't so Lord. Say it ain't so," Jeffrey wailed!

"Jeffrey, what is it," Reesa asked?

"Damn..., she told me all about it a month ago. I need a moist towelette. I think I'm about to pass out," Jeffrey cried.

"Jeffrey. What is wrong," Reesa asked?

"My 9 o'clock appointment is Mrs. Debra Moore," Jeffrey shouted, before he fell to the floor.

HOOP'S TRUTH

Truth is-- Reesa's got daddy issues. She's a smart, sexy and savvy businesswoman. She lost her virginity when she was twenty-five to a forty-five- year-old married man. Her ass ain't been right since. She wants a husband and a family; but she keeps falling for the same type of men-cheaters!

Teresa Weatherspoon, Director of Player and Franchise Development for New York Liberty, played point guard for eight seasons in the WNBA and the first seven with the Liberty. She won an Olympic Gold Medal in the 1988 Olympic Games in Seoul, South Korea and a Bronze Medal in 1992 in Barcelona, Spain.

She served as the Head Basketball Coach of the Louisiana Tech Lady Techsters.

2

Keep My Name Out Your Mouth

Sherman Oaks, California/ Jillian & Angela

It had been months since Jillian dared to brave driving on the freeway during the day; but there she was. For an hour and forty five minutes she drove up the long, mountainous road that led down to the Valley-the 405. She needed answers and today would be the day.

Jillian took the Ventura Boulevard exit. She and a college girlfriend scheduled a lunch date. They were also meeting to discuss a pressing matter. She drove her SUV into a quiet cul-de-sac where her trusted friend, Dr. Angela Colon lived. She parked in front of the house and walked toward the back.

She sighed with relief at the sight of their special meeting place. Jillian, Angela and a few others nicknamed it "The Veranda." Covered by layers of climbing Lonicera vines, the screened veranda, primarily served as Angela's back sunroom.

However, on occasions like this, it also served as a therapy office.

registered into California State Dominquez Hills in Carson instead! No offense; but hello….," Jillian shouted! Jillian tossed her nose in the air and rolled her big green eyes.

"There is absolutely nothing wrong with Cal State! It's an accredited state college! An education is an education. Whether it's learned and earned in a classroom, at a community college, online or in prison. I can't believe you haven't learned about what happens when people judge others. It's a lesson that could keep you out of trouble. Like Mi Abuela used to say "**a hard head makes a soft behind.**"

In other words, remember a lesson learned the first time so it doesn't come back and kick your ass again! Listen, the bottom line is that you both are college educated women-we all are," Angela declared!

"Well, I'm married. And she's not! And my children have the same father," Jillian shouted!

"Whoa! You're hitting below the belt. Leave the kids out of this Jill, Angela said.

Jillian stood when she wanted to get her point across. She stood and crossed her arms.

"I've worked my ass off to become a public figure in my community! And how dare she say that after me being a stay- at-home wife and mother for more than 15 years, that the only way I could have managed to secure this new position was by using "closed- door" knee service tactics!

She even said that I doctored my resume and rubbed elbows with some old men to get my position. I am the President of the Jack and Jill Ladera Heights Chapter! If this gets out, it could ruin everything for me. I mean, if this gets out, it could ruin everything for me and my family," Jillian shouted!

A calm and nonchalant Angela asked, "Are you sure she said that?"

"Yes, I'm sure that South Central Hood Rat, bitch, said it," Jillian screamed!

Jillian drank two flutes of champagne. She cried and complained. She searched frantically through her purse for tissue. She couldn't find any. She settled instead for the napkins that were placed beneath the slices of Entemann's coffee cakes on the table. She was so worked up that she didn't see the box of tissue on the end table next to her champagne flute.

"Something about this doesn't sound right! I mean Keisha may be a little rough around the edges; but she's not mean spirited. How do you know she said it for sure," Angela asked once more?

"Here's the deal Ang. A Soror heard her. I guess you could say she was doing a little **ear hustling** at one of our sorority affairs," Jillian said.

"And you believe her," Angela asked?

"I absolutely do! We crossed[1] together. She is older, wiser and is highly respected among the Sorors in our chapter," Jillian defended!

"I know you're not talking about that same "Old Mighty Isis" Soror lady that you complained to me about when you were on line. Ha! No ma'am, not the one who you said seemed to still be holding on to a grudge she had during her undergraduate days back in the 1990's!

If she's the person that repeated this to you, I would question her motives. Besides, if you all belong to the same organization, local chapter and believe in the same principles, then what is the damn problem," Angela asked?

"Yes, we are; but I must admit, there are times that *not every Soror* behaves or regards others as they should," Jillian replied.

"Now that's interesting and certainly unfortunate. Don't you have a sister code or something? You know I was in the Girls Scouts. We had a code," Angela teased.

"Yes Angela, I've heard all about the Girls Scouts Code of

---

[1] 1.A term used when members of Greek organizations complete initiation with others at the same time. 2.Abuela, grandmother in Spanish.

Honor! And for your concern my sorority has a code of conduct; but people are people! And that's why I'm here talking things over with you, my dear friend," Jillian said slowly and sarcastically.

"Seriously, you two have been close for years. I would hate for your friendship and sisterhood to end over something that may not be true. The two of you should talk and hash things out. Let's keep it one hundred Chica when you talk about singled mothers. We all know that you and Bradley dated for more than seven years before he proposed.

And we all know that your beautiful, elaborate and expensive wedding was also a shotgun wedding," Angela said.

Jillian stood to her feet slowly, folded her slim pecan arms and stared coldly at Angela before uttering, "Fact, Bradley and I got married and we still are," Jillian replied.

"True. That is absolutely true," Angela said.

Jillian then ran her perfectly manicured nails through her short, blonde, wavy, hair and placed her hands on her waist.

She then declared, "I should watch what I say and not judge huh? One thing I can say for certain about myself is- I didn't turn out to be a singled woman, renting a two-bedroom, apartment, filled with toys, junk, and fake ass leather furniture, thinking I'm cute wearing those puffy Janet Jackson braids from Poetic Justice and raising three children by three baby daddies like her! All I know is that she needs to keep my name, Mrs. Jillian Chanel Logan OUT HER MOUTH! She is nothing more to me than a baby making hater. And as far as I'm concerned, Keisha can kiss my pretty ass," Jillian shouted!

HOOP'S TRUTH

Truth-- is-everyone goes to Angela for advice; particularly Jillian. Angela is an Anesthesiologist at Cedars-Sinai Medical Center in Los Angeles and trains UCLA medical students from her office in Santa Monica. In her personal life, she's a fun-loving, smack-talking, Puerto Rican from the Bronx; but to her friends, she's their resident psychologist. She's on call to everyone 24/7!

Lisa Leslie attended the University of Southern California. She played eleven seasons with the Los Angeles Sparks. She was the first player to dunk in a WNBA game.

Leslie is Head Coach for Triplets, an American men's 3-on-3 basketball team that plays in the BIG3. She is also a studio analyst for Orlando Magic broadcasts on Fox Sports Florida.

"Everyone talks about age, but it's not about age. It's about work ethic. Winning never gets old." -Lisa Leslie

3

Who Needs an Escort?

Los Angeles, California/Dr. Angela Colon and Mr. & Mrs. Bergher

Hellen Weaver is a happy-go-lucky, singled, cat owner. For the past ten years she's worked as Dr. Colon's lead Anesthetist at the Cedars Sinai Medical Center.

Over the past three months, she's taken online Spanish classes; but she's doubted her ability to use what she's learned in public. She is however, willing to show her friends at work what she's learned. This morning, before she left for work, she promised her cat Miracle that she'd practice speaking Spanish all day.

Dr. Colon had three colonoscopies scheduled for the day. Her last colonoscopy is scheduled for 11:00 a.m. That appointment was scheduled several months prior. The patient was flagged as priority. It was the doctor's responsibility to discuss any and all concerns with the family of a priority patient before a procedure.

Dr. Colon lives up to her stellar reputation of being thorough, efficient and caring without trying. Last night, while speaking with the patient's wife, she assured that the routine, outpatient procedure would be handled with extra care.

Dr. Colon exited the elevator on the 5th floor. She hurried toward the back entrance of her office. She placed her laptop and coffee mug on her desk as she settled in.

Nurse Hellen busied herself in a neighboring examining room. When she realized the doctor had arrived, she charged into the doctor's office and shouted,

"Hola Señorita[2], Colon!"

The "Boogie Down" Bronx native was unstartled. The doctor's nose was buried deep in patient files. She took a few gulps of coffee before looking up and greeting Nurse Hellen.

"Buenos Dias.[3] You're still working on your Spanish, I see," she said.

"Si,[4]" Nurse Hellen replied.

"Good. Work on it later! We've got work to do. Has the first patient arrived and have they been prepped," Dr. Colon asked?

"Yes, doctor," Nurse Hellen replied.

Nurse Hellen retrieved notes from her desk. She returned to the doctor's office with various documents and a list of the patient discharge approvals for the day.

"Great! This won't take long. I've got to be out of here earlier than normal today," Dr. Colon said.

"For what, a hot date," Nurse Hellen asked?

"Uh… is that any of your business," Dr. Colon snapped.

"No. I just remember that you'd leave early like this when you and Malcolm were together. I'm sorry doctor," Nurse Hellen said.

"It's okay. I understand Hellen.

"Hellen, who are we releasing Mr. Bergher to after his procedure,"

Dr. Colon asked?

"Does he have an escort," the doctor asked loudly?

---

2 Spanish for hello, Miss
3 Spanish for good morning
4 Spanish for yes

"Uh, yes, Dr. Colon he has an escort! That's for sure. She signed his forms and has already fallen asleep on the couch in the waiting area," Nurse Hellen mumbled.

"Good! There will be no malpractice suits on my watch. Let's get to work, Chica,[5]" Dr. Colon said.

"Dr. Colon, There's. And. We should," was all Nurse Hellen said before they were interrupted by office staff and patients.

Meanwhile, at Mountain Maverick Studios in Burbank, California.

Sara Bergher, a studio executive and entertainment mogul, is battling industry executives on a conference call.

She's **fighting tooth and nail** to get the other executives to agree with her. She believes that the star power of the studio's leading man matched with the fresh face and talent of a new female actress, promises to be a box office hit.

"Mrs. Bergher, I'm so sorry to interrupt; but TMZ has just reported that one of our client's is held up in a... Here's my iPad. Take a look," Taylor, her personal assistant said.

"I don't care what TMZ is reporting! Get that client's manager on the line now! Tell him to drag that ungrateful piece of shit out of that pigsty and put him into his car. Then drive to the nearest gas station," Mrs. Bergher screamed!

"And what should they do after that Mrs. Bergher," Taylor asked?

"They'll text you. "You'll send an SUV and off they go," Mrs. Bergher said.

"Uh, to where," Taylor nervously asked?

"Arizona! You're going too! They both have to stay out of trouble and away from the paparazzi until we think of something. Don't worry about luggage. You'll enjoy the drive.

And Taylor, you're still on the clock. Which means, if I don't

---

[5] Spanish for girl

have a contract emailed to me by 12 noon tomorrow for the "Mary Hartman Mary Hartman" reboot, you'll be on permanent leave", Mrs. Bergher shouted!

"Yes, Mrs. Bergher. I'll get on it right away." Taylor replied.

Taylor exited the office and Sara Bergher returned to the conference call. Minutes later, Sara received an internal call from her administrative assistant, Jane.

"Mrs. Bergher, your Nanny is on line two," Jane announced.

"Is the house on fire," Mrs. Bergher asked?

"No? I don't believe so Mrs. Bergher. Would you like me to find out," Jane asked?

"Did anyone die," Mrs. Bergher asked?

"Oh my Mrs. Bergher. I don't know," Jane said as if she were about to cry.

"Then hang up," Mrs. Bergher shouted!

"With all due respect, Mrs. Bergher she sounds concerned and keeps repeating that it's very, very important. What would you like me to do? I can also hear loud noises in the background," Jane reported.

"Well in that case, patch her through. Olga, what the hell do you want," Mrs. Bergher asked?

"Señora⁶ Bergher! Your husband, he's…," Olga shouted!

"He's what? Is he dead? What are you talking about Olga," Mrs. Bergher asked?

"Oh, no! He's alive; but he came home with three verry, verry, verry… young women. They skinny and no clothes hardly on. They look like ladies of the night," Olga whispered.

"What? Speak up! Olga I swear you've got to stop binge watching those 1930's movies. And these young women you've just described sound like prostitutes. That's what they're called now Olga prostitutes! Now what do you want me to do," Mrs. Bergher asked?

---

⁶ Spanish for older woman.

"It's your husband. I think he is verry, verry, verry drunk," Olga added.

"Just keep the women away from the main house. I'll deal with my dear husband later," Mrs. Bergher said.

"They are in the pool now. And the dogs are barking and running wild," Olga shouted!

"Well ya might as well let the dogs have some fun too. After all, **nobody wants a bone, but a dog**. I'm working, Olga. Goodbye," Mrs. Bergher shouted!

"What if they are still here when the kids come home," Olga asked?

"I'll handle the kids. Goodbye," Mrs. Bergher said.

Hours later Sara returned to her home in Calabasas. It was quiet. Erick sat quietly on the couple's bed reading articles on Variety. com on his iPad. Sara joined him on the bed. The two exchanged a loving kiss. Sara took a deep breath and prepared herself.

"Erick, can you explain how three hookers found their way to our home and are still outside by the pool," Sara asked?

"Oh really? Well I don't know," Erick said.

Sara wanted to raise her voice; but she managed not to.

"There are rainbow colored streaks on the front hood of the car and all over the back seat. Tell me Erick, who spray-painted my Bentley," she asked?

"Why would someone do that Sara," Erick asked?

Sara jumped to her feet and walked around to Erick's side of the bed. She stopped suddenly. She took a few more deep breaths; but this time the calming affect didn't work. Her face reddened and she yelled out.

"Goddammit Erick, what the hell happened today," Sara asked?

"Well, I was scheduled for the colonoscopy at 11 a.m. Darling, the rest is a blur," Erick replied.

"Jeffrey tells a different story," Sara shouted!

Jeffrey is the Bergher family's personal house manager. He is a stately, loyal and trustworthy gentleman. However, Erick has been particularly annoyed by Jeffery's mere presence.

"Well I'm glad Jeffrey knows what happened. Hopefully, he can help us get to the bottom of this," Erick replied.

"You're damn right. Right at the bottom of a lake is exactly where you'll be if you don't stop this behavior," Sara said.

"What did you say? My hearing aid must have gone out," Erick said.

"Well change the batteries Erick," Sara quipped.

"I can hear you now. Who are those young girls out by the pool," Erick asked?

"Jeffrey told me all about how you tricked him into thinking he would drive you to Dr. Colon's this morning; but instead you drove off in my Bentley. This was after he found several empty prescription bottles strewn across the kitchen counter," Sara said.

Erick, now confronted with a few facts from the day's events, seemed to ignore or not hear Sara.

"Is Olga going to prepare something for them to eat? Those girls look like they haven't eaten in days. Darling, you must believe me. I don't know what happened after the colonoscopy," Erick said.

"Erick, as crazy as this looks and sounds, I do believe you. You did it again," Sara said.

"Did what," Erick asked?

"You mixed your medications again, didn't you," Sara asked?

"Sara! Tell me I didn't do that again," Erick said.

Sara climbed back on the bed and lied next to her husband. They held each other and sat quietly for a moment.

"Sweetheart, can we rehire Jeffrey as your personal assistant and driver," Sara asked?

"Okay, just as long as he doesn't snoop around while I'm taking a bath. You know what happened the last time," Erick said.

"Yes, I do sweetheart. He found you slumped over in the bathtub. He resuscitated you after you mixed your blood pressure, liver and antidepressant medications. He saved your life Erick," Sara said.

"He did, didn't he? I'll have to thank him for that," Erick replied.

"This can't be. You're only 55," Sara mumbled.

"Come again. What did you say, Sara," Erick asked?

Sara brushed Erick's hair with her hands and kissed his head.

"Erick, what is your name," Sara asked?

"What a silly question," Erick said.

"My name is Erick Bergher, the founder and CEO of Mountain Maverick

Studios," he said.

"Yes Erick. You are the love of my life. Get some rest. I'll call Dr. Colon's office later," she said.

Jeffrey managed to escort the three women back to an area in Los Angeles without the twins noticing. By 8:30 p.m. the twins had eaten dinner, completed their homework, bathed and were put to bed. Sara decided to call Dr. Colon's office Monday morning.

4

In Sickness and In Health

Santa Monica, California/ Dr. Angela Colon & Bradley Logan

Dr. Angela Colon sat alone in her private office reviewing patient files while she waited for a visitor. The office bell rang. It was Bradley Logan.

A nervous Bradley entered.

"Jillian is suspicious. I don't think I can hide it any longer," Bradley said.

"Slow down. Are we talking about your marriage? Or are we talking about what you came here for," Angela asked?

"Well both," Bradley said.

"Bradley, why don't you sit down," Angela suggested.

Bradley sat in a chair at the receptionist desk.

"What do you mean by suspicious," Angela asked?

"She's starting to complain," Bradley shouted!

"Well what is Jillian complaining about now," Angela asked?

"She wants sex! I haven't touched her in months," Bradley said.

"Well that's normal for what you're going through," Angela said.

"I've tried to explain; but she doesn't take anything that I say seriously," Bradley shouted!

"Brad, try to calm down. This has been going on for too long. If you don't tell her, I will," Angela shouted!

"No! It's got to come from me. This is my life," Bradley shouted!

HOOP'S TRUTH

Truth is-- Sara Bergher is a shrewd Hollywood executive. Born and raised in Brooklyn, NY, she will go to the ends of the Earth to keep her family and marriage intact. She has a big mouth, a big wallet and an even bigger heart. She and Erick have been married for 30 years. They were each other's first love. Early dementia has plagued Erick's family for many generations. They are large contributors to several non-profit organizations, such as Autism Speaks. The organization is dedicated to promoting solutions across the spectrum and throughout the lives of individuals with autism and their families. This organization helps me too and so does my uncle Bradley Logan, who happens to be an attorney for the Bergher family. He and Angela have a secret and boy is it a big one!

5

Rumor Has It

Global Creative, North Hollywood /Keisha

On the backlot of Global Creative Studios, producers escorted on golf carts, trucks loaded with crafts services and various talent buzz about in normal fashion. While executives, in offices benched high on hills where only mountain lions can find them, cut deals to make their bag and superstars.

"Global Creative this is Keisha speaking. How may I direct your call? One moment, I'll patch you through," she said.

Keisha Turner is an administrative casting assistant for one of Global Creative's leading producers. She is a college graduate and a mother of three. She is proud of her race and is able to consciously navigate between two worlds daily. Keisha has been a trusted employee for Global Creative for more than 20 years. The studio executives love her professionalism and black power edge.

Keisha received a text message. It was her friend Abeba.

"What does this bougie heifer want now," she thought.

The text read, "Drinks in Toluca Lake at 7 p.m. @NoHo Bar Zone."

Keisha was a bit suspicious. However, she knew that wherever Abeba goes men and the media were sure to follow.

"Wait a minute. That ho owes me some money. After all those "A" list events that I've gotten her into, audition leads and the casting breakdowns that I risked stealing for her? Hmm. Yeah, I'll meet her after work alright," she thought.

Keisha texted back, "Hey girl. See you there Keesh."

"Umm hmm; but **every shut eye ain't sleep**. Instagram, here I come," Keisha said.

Meanwhile, Abeba is seated at the bar in one of her favorite watering holes.

It's been 20 years of struggle and Abeba has finally gotten her first big break. Soon she will become Hollywood's latest "It Girl." She is a stunningly beautiful Ethiopian actress. She has an alluring amber brown skin tone and shoulder length, wavy black hair.

Abeba and a male regular were the only patrons in the restaurant. The staff worked around them as they prepared for happy hour. Abeba is sharing her good news with the bartender.

"A two picture deal. Honey you're gonna be rich," Lucy shouted! Abeba!

"Thanks Lucy. I didn't think I'd get it. Sometimes you guys believe in me more than I believe in myself," Abeba said.

"You're talented and a natural beauty. It was just a matter of time," the male patron said.

"Yeah; but sometimes not even talent can help you book a gig in Hollywood. Nobody knows how hard it's been. And how much I've lost trying to fulfill my dreams," Abeba replied.

"Listen, I've been working all over Hollywood since the 1960's. I've seen and heard all of the stories. Many of the greats have drowned their sorrows right here. And some of their photos are on these walls in this restaurant. Your regular is on me today sweetheart," Lucy said.

"No thanks Lucy. I'll have two bottles of champagne. Today I'm celebrating with a friend," Abeba said.

"Coming up superstar," Lucy replied.

Keisha secured parking at the restaurant before its valet parking had begun. She sat in her Jeep Wrangler and did a quick hair, makeup, wardrobe and confidence check before getting out.

"Altoids. Check. Lip gloss. Check. I've got my cellphone and my braids are nice and tight. I hope this ain't no swingers club on the low. Okay, here goes," Keisha thought.

Abeba spotted Keisha immediately. She called out to Keisha in her distinct Oromo accent. The Oromo language is an Afro-asiatic dialect spoken by Ethiopians from Kenya within the Oromia region which is - Abeba's homeland.

"Hey there My Love," Abeba shouted!

"Hey Abeba. It's good to see you," Keisha said.

"Send the bottles to our table please," Abeba instructed a waiter.

"Well damn, girl. Can we get to a table first," Keisha asked?

"Keisha we already have a table," Abeba said.

"Okay, well why are we sitting here," Keisha asked?

Abeba closed her eyes, inhaled deeply then exhaled. She repeated this exercise three times as Keisha sat quietly and looked on.

Afterward, Abeba took Keisha's hands and looked her in the eyes. Keisha interrupted and said, "Abeba, what's up girl? " I want to refocus your energy Keisha," Abeba said.

"Girl is this why you invited me here, to watch you breathe," Keisha asked?

"No. I have good news. And I want to celebrate it with you; but before we do, we need to shift our energy. Can you breathe with me Keisha," Abeba asked?

For two seconds Keisha and Abeba sat with their eyes closed as they breathed and refocused their energy. When they opened their eyes, the waiter was standing nearby. He led them to their table.

The table had been set with a bouquet of fresh violets. Added to the display of celebratory decadence were two bottles of G.H. Mumm Champagne, two Arturo Fuente Opus X cigars, an assortment of cheeses, bread and hors d'oeuvres.

"Wow! What are we celebrating," Keisha asked?

"I just booked a two picture deal with Mountain Maverick Studios! Gimme some," Abeba shouted!

Abeba and Keisha gave one another a high five.

"Wow! Now that's what I'm talking about! I'm so happy for you," Keisha said.

"I'm happy for me, too," Abeba shouted!

"Who is your co-star," Keisha asked?

"I can't reveal that now. They're still in negotiations," Abeba replied.

"Well can you tell me the name of the film," Keisha asked?

"It's called "Ko-Thi." It's from the Sherbro language of Sierra Leone meaning seek and embrace black culture. That's all I can tell you." Abeba said.

"It sounds quite interesting; but you know that's some bullshit not telling me who your co-star is. You do remember who I work for and that I can find out for my damn self? Anyway, looks like you'll be traveling out of the country soon," Keisha said.

"Absolutely," Abeba shouted!

"Just make sure you control yourself; particularly if you'll be gone for an extended amount of time," Keisha advised.

"Cheers to me and my co-star," Abeba teased.

"Cheers! As long as the champagne is flowing, I'll have all the information that I need before dessert. Woo hoo! Abeba," Keisha shouted!

"Keisha, I want to ask you something; but you have to give me your word, that you won't take it the wrong way," Abeba said.

"That depends. As long as you don't ask me to participate in that freaky swinger stuff that you're into," Keisha said.

"No Keisha. I can't believe that you even talk that way; particularly after having children. My Love, are you afraid to be free? I mean sexually free," Abeba asked?

"What? My sex ain't for free," Keisha yelled!

"Please don't get defensive! That's not what I'm saying. Why don't you give yourself permission to be pleasured the way you want and as often as you'd like," Abeba asked?

"And why don't you stop trying to turn me into a ho? I'm not like you," Keisha scoffed!

"Keisha, how can you be sweet one minute and then a trash-talking banjee girl[7] the next? What's up with the attitude," Abeba asked?

"I'm sorry. That was totally uncalled for. I'm working on a huge project at work and I'm stressed," Keisha replied.

"Really Keesh," Abeba asked?

"Yeah," Keisha replied.

"The way you just snapped at me something else is going on! You're too young for menopause. Are you pregnant again," Abeba grilled?

"No," Keisha refuted!

"Are you depressed," Abeba grilled again?

"No dammit! Will you get on with the question," Keisha demanded!

"You're bipolar! That's okay. I know plenty of bipolar people. Which meds do you take? Spill it Keisha," Abeba said.

"It's not that! One of my children's fathers is getting married. And he asked Justin if he'd like to be in the wedding," Keisha replied.

"Oh. I'm sorry Keesh; but which one of your baby daddies is getting married, Abeba asked?

---

[7] an offensive term used to describe urban girls as being ghetto.

"Didn't I say Justin," Keisha snarled.

"Girl, you've got Jayden, James and Justin. Excuse me if I don't remember their father's names. Give me a break," Abeba said.

"Justin is Daniel's son," Keisha replied.

"Oh, your oldest," Abeba said.

"Yes," Keisha said.

"Oh, I see. Keisha. I know this may be difficult for you; but did you ever think about what you would do when and if he ever got married," Abeba asked?

"I guess it ran across my mind; but I never put much thought into it until now. Honestly, I never thought it would actually happen," Keisha said.

"Justin is seventeen years old. Have you been hoping to reconcile with Daniel all this time," Abeba asked?

"He was my first love," Abeba," Keisha said.

Keisha began to cry. Abeba reached for a tissue from her mini clutch.

"You need more work than I thought. We've got to make a list of things to do," Abeba said.

"Say what," Keisha said as she blew her nose.

"There are plenty of people who idolize their first loves or ex this or that. Only to find out later that what they thought they were was just an illusion. By the time the two of them get to know one another as adults, one or both of them realize that they have absolutely nothing in common. Let's eat. I'll give you the number to one of my therapists," Abeba said.

"Well, damn. How many do you have," Keisha asked?

"Only three," Abeba replied.

"Only three," Keisha shouted!

"Yes, My Love. One therapist can't fix all of this. One helps me with my sex addiction. Another with my adoption issues and the other helps me through my anxieties about everything else.

I'm not worried about this little eating disorder thing that pops up every now and then," Abeba said.

"Sex addiction? Okay, so when you hook up with these random men on the set, at restaurants, at Ralphs Supermarket and at the clubs, you're actually acting out because of an addiction," Keisha asked?

"Yes, I'm a nymphomaniac and I can't control myself," Abeba replied.

"Wow! I didn't know. I apologize for judging you and calling you a ho all these years. How long have you known," Keisha asked?

"It's okay. I was diagnosed about eight months ago. Things were really getting out of control and I knew I needed professional help," Abeba said.

"You can say that again. Keisha mumbled. I'm just happy you're getting the help you need," she said.

"Keesh! Some muscular eye candy just walked in. He's on your right. Get his attention! Unbutton your blouse a little. More! And please take that scrunchie off. Let your hair down," Abeba insisted.

Keisha did as Abeba instructed. She turned to her right and stole a glance at a tall, dark and handsome man who looked to be in his mid to late 40's.

"Oh, yes! He is fine. What is his race," Keisha asked?

"It shouldn't matter. Perk your girls up to get his attention. Don't be scared, unbutton another button! Add buy new bras on your "to do" list too," Abeba said.

"I guess I should take tips from you more often," Keisha said.

"Why not, I'm your friend and beauty is my business," Abeba said.

"I've needed a makeover for the longest; but I was too embarrassed to ask for help. You really live up to your name. You maybe a little wacky, but your spirit is beautiful just like the Ethiopian flower," Keisha said.

"Okay, enough. When was the last time you had sex," Abeba asked?

"Five years ago," Keisha whispered.

"Add that to the list too. I know some people who can help you," Abeba said.

"Abeba, this is going too far! You really *are* trying to turn me into a ho," Keisha yelled!

"That is not my intention. I just happen to know a few guys that are willing to service women in need," Abeba said.

"I have never paid for the D and *I ain't gonna pay for it* now," Keisha declared!

Both Abeba and Keisha were tipsy and feeling really happy. Abeba was still smoking her cigar. Keisha got dizzy after inhaling and put hers out.

"Weren't you supposed to ask me something," Keisha asked?

"Oh yeah, we've been friends for about five years and Angela and Jillian have been friends since college. Before I go on, I need you to promise me that you will remain calm," Abeba slurred.

"Stop beating around the bush," Keisha said.

"Hollywood is a beast. And none of us could have maintained our sanity if it wasn't for our bond and friendship. A rumor has been circulating and I'm worried that it will lead to a huge blowout," Abeba said.

"Well, what the hell does that have to do with me? Damn is Jillian still denying that we used to drive to Mexico to buy diet pills? That's the only thing that I've shared," Keisha said.

"No silly. I'm just asking everyone to be mindful of what we share about each other's personal lives. We're sisters and trust should never be an issue. The next bottle is on you," Abeba said.

"Oh, Lord. You've got my boobs out and my hair down. Now you've turned me into a cleavage exposing, drunk and lying ho," Keisha slurred and clowned.

"You might get lucky tonight," Abeba teased.

HOOP'S TRUTH

Truth is-- therapy is beneficial. Mama wished that I started my treatment for Asperger's much sooner. I see a therapist regularly and there are support groups for caregivers and parents held at my counseling center. Abeba has three therapists. She's a talented, free spirited earthchild. Keisha wishes she could attract men as Abeba does; but she's sexually rigid and militant. Keisha once used her multiple pregnancies as a financial security blanket. Both women are lovable and want love. Both have been or are promiscuous, have handled rejection poorly and are prone to engage in behaviors such; as stalking and or damaging the property of their ex-lovers. Both could benefit from attending therapy to learn how to love themselves first and unconditionally.

6

Not A Priority

Los Angeles,California/ Bradley & Jillian Logan

Bradley Logan is a corporate attorney and is married with three children. The family lives in a beautiful home in Ladera Heights. It's an upscale neighborhood that's nestled closely to "the jungle," an area heavily shaded by tropical trees and foliage.

Bradley is at home speaking with his father on the phone. His parents are concerned about the state of their son's marriage.

"I don't know dad. At first our married seemed perfect. I don't know where things went wrong? We just grew apart. No! No! There is no other woman. What do you mean **it's cheaper to keep her?**

It's just not working out. She's too busy being miss everything to everybody. Our marriage is not a priority. I'm not a priority! Yes, we've been in therapy for months; but it's not working, dad! She's home now!

Jillian has arrived home. Her SUV is parked in the driveway. Bradley rushed out of the house to meet her.

"Where is he? He knew I was bringing groceries home. Ugh," Jillian grumbled.

"Hey babe," Bradley said.

Jillian's head was deep within the tailboard of her SUV.

They walked into the kitchen and dropped the groceries on the island counter. They unloaded the groceries together as they did normally.

"Thank you," Jillian said.

"Why are you thanking me? We do this all the time," Bradley said.

"Did I? My mind is **running a mile a minute**. How was your day Brad," Jillian asked?

"It was okay. Ah did we forget something," Bradley asked?

"Oh, kiss," Jillian said.

"I thought you'd never ask," Bradley replied.

Bradley pulled Jillian close and kissed her. He held onto to her and stared into her eyes.

Jillian pulled away. "Okay, okay, okay Brad," Jillian said.

"Well I've missed you today too," Bradley said.

"I missed you today Bradley. Is that what you'd like to hear," Jillian asked?

"How was your day babe," Bradley asked?

"Long," Jillian replied.

"Is that it? What else? I see it written all over your face," Bradley said.

"Are you sure you want to know? I'll start and then you'll drift off. Besides, this is girl talk anyway. I'll just call Reesa later. It's almost nine o'clock in New York. She should be home from the salon in another hour," Jillian said.

"Jillian, you've shared the drama about your Sorors and girlfriends with me for years. What's bothering you," Bradley asked?

Jillian slammed a can of tomatoes on the counter. "It's that ghetto, hating-ass Keisha! A Soror heard her say that I doctored my resume and," Jillian said.

"Come on. That sounds ridiculous," Bradley said.

"She also implied that I used **closed door tactics** to get my job at Jack and Jill," Jillian shouted!

"Like what?" Bradley asked,"

"How should I know, Bradley? She's lying," Jillian screamed!

"Why would Keisha say that," Bradley asked?

"She's jealous of my life! I mean she's jealous of our life," Jillian screamed!

"I think you should consider the source. Why would one of your sorority sisters come to you with something negative that another sister supposedly said about you? Not to mention this is Keisha we're talking about. You two are sorority sisters and have been friends since high school. For God's sake we're Justin's godparents. Don't worry yourself about this. It's hard enough starting your career after raising our kids. I want you to know that you've got my full support; the same way that you've supported me," Bradley said.

"I love you Bradley. Thank you for supporting me through graduate school and supporting me now. You're right honey. I'll talk to her one on one soon okay," Jillian said.

"Good. Jill? There's something that I…" Bradley said.

Jillian interrupted. She grabbed her appointment book and cellphone.

"Omg! How could I have forgotten? James has a varsity game tonight. You're going, right? Where is John? Oh, he's studying at the library with his nerdy friends and… dammit, I've got to take Jasmine to ballet in a half hour. You were saying," Jillian asked?

"Never mind, Jillian. You're not listening," Bradley said.

"I am listening," Jillian shouted!

"Jillian please put your phone down-this is important," Bradley said.

"I'm just forwarding this email to the Sorors. I can hear you Bradley," Jillian replied as she continued to text.

"I think we should separate," Bradley said.

"Please let me know your thoughts. Love Soror Logan," Jillian mumbled.

"I said, I think we should separate," Bradley shouted!

"What did I tell you about thinking Bradley? Besides we haven't finished our couple's therapy homework," Jillian said.

"There's no need for us to finish it Jill," Bradley said.

"Great timing Brad. It's just like you to pull a selfish move like this; as soon as I become the Chapter President of Jack and Jill. Perfect," Jillian shouted!

"It's all about you," Bradley said.

"Don't come for me Bradley! For more than 25 years its' been all about you! You're the one who wanted a successful business, children and a stay-home-wife," Jillian shouted!

Bradley grabbed his coat and keys and walked toward the kitchen door.

"On second thought, I want a divorce," Bradley shouted as he stormed out the kitchen door.

"Ha! I worked too hard for this life. And I ain't going nowhere," Jillian said.

HOOP'S TRUTH

"Truth is-- Bradley is educated, charming, fine as hell and comes from a wealthy family. Jillian is a social climber and has always manipulated people with her beauty and charm. However, she has been a dutiful wife and mother. Bradley is a bit of a Mama's boy and has always believed that his marriage should be exactly as his parents. Jillian loves Bradley; but she feels that she's never lived her own life. She regrets getting married at a young age. The new job will be an outlet for her. She views it as her time to shine and to enjoy financial independence. However, she would never think of parting ways with her marital status and assets; even if meant forsaking everyone's happiness.

7

Baby Love

Marina Del Rey / Malcolm & Angela

Malcolm hoped the ambience of the ocean, yachts, and the restaurant's décor would help to impress Angela. He desperately wants to regain her trust.

His business in construction management had grown and he was ready to build a future with the woman that he truly loved. Angela agreed to meet him for lunch at the Warehouse Waterfront Restaurant. It had been three years since their break up.

"Can I get a hug," Malcolm asked?

"Hello Malcolm. Why are we here," Angela asked?

"It was time," Malcolm said.

"Time for what," Angela asked?

"Time for us to stop acting like we're not meant for each other. I miss you and I want to make things right," Malcolm said.

"Whatever," Angela replied.

"Whatever? You must be seeing someone, huh? I saw him," Malcolm said.

"What? Who?" Angela asked?

"I saw that Mercedes Benz that was parked late one night at your office," Malcolm said.

"I'm a doctor, Malcolm. That's where my patients see me. Does that make sense? No, this is you speculating and deflecting. Besides, what the hell were you doing outside my office," she asked?

"Are you seeing him or was he a patient," Malcolm asked?

"Not that it's any of your business; but the answer is no! I am not seeing anyone. Many of my patients drive expensive cars Malcolm! We're done here," Angela said.

"I'm sorry. I just needed to see you that night to ask you then; but I didn't want to scare you. It's been too long. I wanted to do it the right way. Are we okay," Malcolm asked?

"What about that woman you moved in with right after we broke up," Angela asked?

"It's over. I was confused. You had a career and I was just. I didn't love her. Okay! Are we good," Malcolm asked again?

"Yes, I'm good," Angela replied.

"Yes, I know you're good," Malcolm replied.

"Sex, that's all you want! You've got two more seconds before I leave. The clock is ticking. Go Hombre[8]," Angela shouted!

"No, no! What I mean is you're good to me and for me. We shared a life and I want us to build a better life together," Malcolm said.

Angela began to cry.

"Life! It was my baby. My baby," Angela shouted!

Malcolm placed her hands into his. Tears fell down his face.

"It was our baby Angela," Malcolm said.

"Stop it Malcolm," she whispered.

"You pushed me away. What was I supposed to do," Malcolm asked?

Love me Malcolm. Love me through it! You were supposed to love me through my loss, pain and depression. All I had was you.

---

[8] man

I had no one! My parents were gone. And you. You left me. You were Mi Familia,[9]" Angela shouted!

"Give me a chance to make things right. I never understood that old saying until now. **You never miss the water until your well runs dry.**" I want to **right my wrongs.** Casate. Conmigo [10]Angela," Malcolm asked?

---

[9] My family
[10] Marry me

GLORIA LYNN HOWE

HOOP'S TRUTH

Truth is--Malcolm is a serial "commitment-phobe." When they met, he worked as sub-contracting laborer. Angela had just begun her residency at Cedars Sinai Medical Center. The two moved in together. Malcolm came from a proud family. He wanted to take care of Angela; but he couldn't. Her earning potential far outweighed his. Their relationship was strained. Angela tolerated the inconsistencies in their four year relationship because he was a fine, hardworking black man who was good in bed. Perhaps her main reason for tolerating the ups and downs in their relationship was because her biological clock was ticking. Not to mention the ever- present pressure from her family to be married and have children. After the miscarriage she felt hopeless. Malcolm moved out and moved on with another woman. Soon after, Angela's career took off. Most of Angela's peers at work are married with children. She's deafly afraid of living alone and being labeled as a barren spinster.

8

Karaoke Kray Kray

Gwinnett County, Georgia / Mr. Gerald

Rita hurried to her living room and sat on the futon couch. She placed her laptop to her left and a warm bowl of leftover shrimp fried rice to her right. Shrouded on the worn carpet in front of her was a pack of colored construction paper, a pile of loose-leaf papers, colored markers and sentence strips.

Earlier, she heard a few colleagues say that the superintendent would make a surprise visit to their school the next day. Given the reputation of the school where Rita works, a visit would be likely. She is very close in receiving her tenure license as an English teacher. Each day she is determined to be the **sharpest pencil in the box**.

The phone rang. It was her cousin Neicy. Unlike Rita, Neicy's primary goal in life is to party, post selfies of herself partying and to find a good man at da club. Neicy was recently hired as a correctional officer at the local prison. Rita worries that her cousin may be terminated soon if she doesn't slow down and stop posting her late-night shenanigans.

"She's calling me already? Damn! Her shift just ended. I'm not fooling with her ratchet behind tonight. I may have to impress the superintendent tomorrow," Rita thought.

On the fourth ring, an agitated Rita answered.

It was ten eighteen p.m. when Neicy swiped her identification badge at the exit gate of the Gwinnett County Jail.

"You ready," Neicy asked?

"Huh," Rita said.

"Chil get dressed. I'll be there in fifteen minutes," Neicy replied.

An alarmed Rita stood up quickly. When she stood, her leftovers flew every which way. The sauce spilled on the futon. The fried rice, onions and a few vegetables stained the construction paper and a pile of student work. She'd graded it and planned to display the work on the bulletin board in her class the next morning. She was done!

Angered that her dinner and students work were ruined, Rita was now hell bent on setting boundaries with her cousin. She heard noises coming from the tenants parking area. She tiptoed toward the living room window.

As she moved closer, she recognized the noise as trap music blaring from her cousin Neicy's car. She was really done!

Rita's phone rang again. Rita stepped over the mess as she scrambled to locate her phone. She found it under the bowl on the floor. She wiped it off and answered. It was Neicy calling from outside.

"Rita! You're going right," Neicy asked?

"Absolutely not! I ain't no **street walker** like you. And why are you outside my apartment making all that noise," Rita asked?

"Oh you see me? Well open the door girl! I've got to change out of this uniform. Look, I'm driving, it's free to get in and they've got free food," Neicy said.

"Free food! Well umm...," Rita said.

"Chil stop **hemming and hawing,** your Cuzzo Neicy ain't

gonna **steer you wrong**. It's always poppin on "Wine Down 4 What Wednesdays," Neicy exclaimed!

"Neicy! It's a work night," Rita protested!

"And that's why we're going out because you just got off work and I just got off work and it's time to PARTAY! PARTAY! PARTAY," Neicy shouted!

"Maybe another time Neicy. I've got to finish grading papers. Tomorrow the district superintendent may visit my school and I want to be prepared," Rita explained.

"That's why your ass is sitting in there on my old futon with no man. Rita you need to stop living under a rock and ordering takeout. Come out and have fun. The twins are coming too! And if the Super does visit your raggedy- ass school tomorrow, he damn sure ain't gonna visit your bad-assed class," Neicy declared!

"Its people like you who don't realize all that teachers do! We take our work home physically and mentally. I need my rest! Real teachers don't just clock in and out. Some people take a briefcase or tools home; but we take our students, their work and their family's home daily," Rita shouted!

"Cuzzo please relax. I appreciate all that you do for the "Bey Bey's" kids of America; but Cat Daddy from WQRU is hosting tonight. And I know you love his deep, velvety voice, and those oldies; but goodies that he plays," Neicy said.

"Cat Daddy," Rita shouted!

"Yes gurl," Neicy shouted!

"I can't go. My hair is a mess and I need a touch-up," Rita said.

"Just wear that nice wig that you bought in New York. You might as well since you **paid a pretty penny for it**," Neicy said.

"Yes! The one I bought from Unique Beauty Boutique. Okay, I'm in. I hope they have some hot wings," Rita said.

"Rita, you talking too much. Open the door girl. I gotta go to the bathroom," Neicy shouted!

Thirty minutes later, Rita and Neicy arrived at Peaches Supper Club. Karaoke was featured there each Wednesday night.

The club was located in a rural area in Norcross, Georgia. There was a bar with a DJ booth behind it. The dimly lit room was filled with several tables and a small stage in the back. The club catered to a 40 plus and older crowd. The club was packed. The crowd was a mixture of the young and old; with a handful of the club's weekday lounge lizards.

"That can't be Cat Daddy," Rita exclaimed!

"It sounds like him," Neicy replied.

"He doesn't look anything like the flyers I see around town. I thought he'd be a **tall glass of water**. Not a short, bald piglet," Rita griped.

"Chil he's still jamming," Neicy replied.

"I wonder what's taking the twins so long," Rita said.

"They'll be here. I'll be back. I'm gonna take a picture with Cat Daddy," Neicy said.

She walked off and blended into the crowd dancing and singing. Rita remained at the table enjoying the music and free food.

The twins were ten minutes away at a gas station. They'd been Rita's closest friends since elementary school. Their families were neighbors and looked out for one another in every way.

Marlene and Darlene are identical in appearance; but opposite in personality. Both have an expresso brown skin tone and are tall and thin.

"Hurry up Marlene! We're already late," she begged.

"Darlene the drinks will still be at half price by the time we get there," Marlene replied.

"It's not that. You see that man right there? There's something creepy about him," Darlene whispered.

At the pump ahead of them, was an older man fumbling in the trunk of a 1986 burgundy Ford Taurus. The man wore a pair of burgundy overalls, a burgundy tee shirt, and a pair of burgundy cowboy boots. Around his neck were several thick, shiny gold chains; but what caught Darlene's eyes was the long, wet and shiny jheri curled hair that rested on his shoulders.

"Oh yeah Sis that is creepy. And that jheri curl," Marlene, said.

"Let's get out of here. He looks **throwed off**. I'll keep a close eye on him and reset the GPS while you pump the gas," Darlene said.

Marlene's tank was almost full when the creepy old man approached their car.

"Hey there, Lil ladies. Ooh, ya'll twins. Care for some icecream? Hee hee," the man asked then laughed in a filthy kind of way.

The man did something that both amazed; yet almost frightened the twins to death. They screamed. Then Marlene ran to the driver's side of her car, jumped in and sped off quickly.

Meanwhile, back at da club.

Rita is nursing a Singapore Sling cocktail and flipping through a book of karaoke songs. Neicy is in the middle of the dance floor with her selfie stick recording a Facebook live video. Minutes later, Marlene and Darlene arrived. They located Rita and joined her at the table.

"Hey! "What took ya'll so long," Rita asked?

"We stopped for gas," Darlene said.

"We almost didn't make it," they said.

"What do you mean," Rita asked?

"Gurl I need something strong to drink. I still can't believe what I just saw," Marlene said.

Neicy returned to the table and greeted The Twins.

"What ya'll talking about," she asked?

"Nothing until we get something strong to drink," Marlene declared.

"I got you! Neicy reached into her purse and pulled out a flask and two small cups. She placed her hands under the table and poured a brown drink into the cups. She placed their cups on the table. 'There's your drink. Now tell us what happened," Neicy said.

The twins reluctantly accepted Neicy's concoction. They both took tiny sips, before Marlene proceeded to tell them about their encounter.

"While I was getting gas, there was this creepy old man at the pump in front of my car. He had a long jheri curl and was wearing all burgundy. This fool even wore burgundy cowboy boots," Marlene said.

"What's so creepy about that," Neicy asked?

"He wasn't pumping gas! He was just fumbling in the trunk of this car," Darlene shouted!

"And his trunk was junky as hell! It looked like he had **everything, but the kitchen sink** in it," Marlene shouted!

"I saw him pull out a few blankets and tools. Then he pulled out a huge barrel marked vanilla icecream," Darlene explained.

"Icecream? From the trunk of his car," Rita asked?

"Yes," Marlene and Darlene shouted!

"When my tank was almost full, I saw him walking toward my car. It looked like he had a bottle of something gooey in his hands. His overalls were almost down to his ankles. And before I knew it, he was gyrating and pouring the gooey stuff on his," Marlene said.

Marlene stopped in mid- sentence. She was too embarrassed to describe what she saw.

A curious Neicy interjected and asked the twins if the man was naked from the waist down. Neither twin responded. Instead, Marlene covered her mouth and shook her head.

"And then this fool started singing an old song that we used to jam to back in the day. You would remember it if you heard it," Darlene said.

"Did you see his thing or not," Neicy asked?

"You mean to tell me that this happened at the gas station," Rita asked?

"At the gas station," Marlene and Darlene shouted!

"Umm hmm. Ya'll saw his junk," Neicy said.

"Whatever we saw was pulsating and huge. It almost looked alive. I'm still in shock," Darlene said.

"Damn anaconda forever," Neicy shouted!

"We **hauled ass** out of there," Darlene shouted!

"That's all that happened? That man sounded harmless," Neicy said.

"Rita, how many drinks has she had," Darlene asked?

"Who knows? That's why I stay in the house," Rita said.

"And that's why you ain't getting none," Neicy shouted!

"And you are kray kray Neicy," Rita shouted!

Everyone laughed. Marlene and Darlene finished Neicy's unidentifiable concoction then headed to the bar to buy a legal drink and mingle.

The karaoke segment was about to begin. It was the norm to begin with a regular singer who had vocal skills or some other talent that would encourage the patrons to sing along, buy drinks eat and dance.

Cat Daddy asked the crowd to applaud for the first karaoke singer, Mr. G. He started karaoke off with a party starter, the 1988 R & B classic, "It Takes Two," by Rob Base and DJ E-Z's. Almost immediately, the crowd jumped up and hit the dance floor.

"Oh my goodness! That's Mr. Gerald," Rita shouted!

"Mr. Who," Neicy, asked?

"Mr. Gerald, the head custodian at my school. Lord, please don't let him see me. He'll talk my head off," Rita joked.

"Damn, grandpa's got bars," Neicy shouted!

"Shhh! I said I didn't want him to see me," Rita scolded.

Just about everyone in the club sang along with Mr. G. And at the end of his song, Mr. G made a beeline to Rita and Neicy's table.

"I must have said it to myself about **50/11 times.** That ain't Ms. Rita Wilson. No it ain't, especially on a school night; but it is you! How ya'll ladies doin," Mr. Gerald asked?

"Fine," they replied.

"Now tell me something I don't know. Hee hee. Miss Rita, why come you don't wear your hair like that at the schoolhouse? It looks nice on your fine, pretty face," Mr. Gerald asked in a repulsive kind of way?

"Umm thank you Mr. Gerald. Uh, we're here with our boyfriends; if you'll excuse us," an annoyed Rita said.

"Oh, I just wanted to say hello. Have a good night," Mr. Gerald said.

The lines were very long at bar. It took Marlene and Darlene almost fifteen minutes to get their drinks.

"My feet hurt already," Darlene complained.

"I've got a pair of flats in my car. Take my keys and I'll take our drinks to the table," Marlene suggested.

Darlene walked out the back door. The club had only two huge outdoor lights; one at the front entrance and the other at the back exit.

Darlene used her cellphone to locate her sister's car. When she found it, she began to rummage under the seats looking for Marlene's flat shoes.

"I can't find these shoes with all this junk in this car," Darlene mumbled.

Just then a man approached Darlene.

"Why come you ain't answer my question earlier," he asked?

"Excuse me? Oh my God! No! Please," Darlene yelled!

Meanwhile, inside da club.

"Ooh that woman could really sing. Marlene, where's your sister" Rita asked?

"Her **dogs were hollerin.** She went to my car to get a pair of flats," Marlene replied.

"She's been gone for a minute. You sure she ain't out there making em," Neicy asked?

By this time Neicy was drunk. Her mind was definitely playing tricks on her. She suspected Darlene of doing something and it was up to her to investigate.

"I bet she met some cute guys and wants to keep em all to herself. I back," Neicy slurred.

"What did she say? Rita she's had too much to drink," Marlene said.

"Neicy, you are a hot mess. Sit down. Don't' go out there and do something foolish! Remember you're still on probation. And Marlene, I don't know how; but ratchet people like my cousin, seem to know how to hold their liquor without missing a day of work. Hurry back before I sing," Rita shouted!

Neicy stumbled her way to the front door. She stood under the front light and yelled Darlene's name several times.

"Darlene! Darlene," she shouted!

A man emerged from the darkness and parked cars.

"Ssir, have you seen a tall woman in a bootiful dress. It's ttt turr turquoise and its bootuful," Neicy asked in a drunken haze?

"Oh, yeah. I saw her over there by that van. Come with me. I'll take you to her," the man said.

"Oh, that's so nice of you. Wait I've got to use the flashlight on my cellphone so I can see better. Burgundy Boots! You're that man from the gas station! And what the hell is that? Help! Help," Neicy shouted!

Back in da the club.

"Rita, you sure have a beautiful voice," Marlene said.

"Thank you, Marlene. I'm glad I came. You know singing is my true passion," Rita replied.

"I'm concerned now. They both have been gone for too long. I'm going out to that parking lot," Marlene declared!

"You shouldn't go alone. We'll both go," Rita shouted!

"No, that's my twin sister! You stay here with our things and if I'm not back in five minutes, come out there and bring that big bouncer over there with you," Marlene demanded!

"Okay, text me as soon as you "**lay eyes on them**," Rita said.

In the back of da club.

At the far end of the parking area was a 1986 burgundy Taurus. The car was parked next to a small wooden shack.

"Now you two pretty Lil ladies stay put and listen to me sang a song. And if ya'll act right I'll take ya back to the house and treat you to some soft and creamy icecream. Hee hee! A one in a million chance of a lifetime," the man sang.

Before leaving the club, Marlene asked a bartender if she could borrow a flashlight. She exited the rear door of the club. Instinctively she walked in the direction of the burgundy Taurus.

As she came closer, she heard a man singing loudly. Then she stepped on something. It was one of her flat shoes. She knew then that something was wrong.

"A one in a million chance of a lifetime," the man howled louder.

"Excuse me, have you... Oh my God, it's you! Where's my sister? Help! Help! Somebody call the law," Marlene screamed!

Marlene fainted and fell to the ground.

Marlene was covered with a blanket and had just come to. It was thirty minutes later and the club was empty. No one was there except, Rita, the club management, the paramedics and the Gwinnett County Police who were completing their investigation.

"How did they get here so fast," Rita asked?

"They were already here. There was a police patrol vehicle parked outside. Everything was caught on an off duty policeman's Dash Cam," the bouncer said.

"Ma'am there was another woman in the trunk. How are you related" an officer asked?

"She's my cousin Denise Cunningham," Rita replied.

"Trunk! Is Darlene okay," Marlene asked?

"They were shaken up a bit. You'll be able to see them soon," an ambulatory technician replied.

"And why is Mr. Gerald in the back of that police car," Rita asked?

"A number of women have been harassed and or abducted from various karaoke clubs throughout the State of Georgia. We have a strong suspicion that he's the man we've been looking for," another officer commented.

Mr. Gerald shouted from the police car, "Ya'll wasn't worth my time, icecream nor my sanging anyway. Ya **Ornery Husseys**!"

HOOP'S TRUTH

Truth is-- Gerald is my father. He's been chasing women and his dream of being a singer for years. My mother left him after I was born. It broke his heart. When I turned three, he sent me to live with his sister in Maryland. He visits us every year. Yeah, he is a bit creepy; but he wasn't always that way. He never got over my mother's rejection. He objectifies women. On the outside he appears to be kind; but on the inside he is a scorned man. He's lonely and wants to be loved. I guess he never learned how to love a woman. I've never met my mother. I often wonder where and who she is?

9

Kitchen Talk

Halethorpe, Maryland /Dorothy Hill, Hoop & James Lewis

The church bellower belted the bells promptly at 8:00 a.m.; as Dorothy, robed in her favorite house coat, sat quietly at her kitchen table. She drank a cup of coffee and jotted down a few things on her "to do" list. Each time the bells rang it was a little reminder of her faith. It gave her a sense of peace, if just for a moment.

Dorothy married Donald Hastings at a tender age. It was sometime during the 1960s. He was a burly man ten years her senior. He was gainfully employed at the Bethlehem Steel Company. Back then, it was a huge deal for a black man to secure full-time employment at the steelmaking and shipbuilding complex. The large industrial site was located just outside of Dundalk, in an unincorporated community in southeastern Baltimore County and was named after its owner, Thomas Sparrow. Donald's work was hard and dangerous; but he did what he had to do to **make ends meet.**

To a young Dorothy, the future looked bright and promising to have married such a strong man with a steady job at Sparrow's

Point. The two lived together in various neighborhoods throughout West Baltimore; a row house in Whitelock, a one- bedroom in Upton and a two-bedroom in one of the high rises of the Murphy Homes Projects.

Five years into their marriage, the couple moved more than six times. Now they were renting a room in a house near the corner of Freemont and Franklin Streets. Dorothy managed to enroll at Coppin State College. Her dream was to become a nurse. Dorothy was determined.

On the other hand, Donald was reaching a boiling point. The physical strain of work and the demand for imported steel was an ever-present and pervasive threat. It seemed nothing could protect him from the avalanche that lied ahead. Each evening he'd return home seemingly less of himself. Things got even worse after his shift was cut. Instead of going home, he *convened on the corner* for hours with others. They'd drink cheap liquor, beer shoot dope and talk about "the man." This became his routine. A routine he preferred over his wife; a routine that became his life.

Donald was no longer the stout and proud man he once was, he'd become a faceless figure amongst a crowd of fractured souls. To this day, pain occupies the corners of West Baltimore streets.

None-the-less, Dorothy never let those obstacles keep her from reaching her goals. She became a fulltime pediatric nurse at the Sacred Hearts Hospital in Baltimore and purchased her first home in 1988. And after serving 40 years as a devoted nurse, the spunky, quick-witted, retiree, had become a mother at the age of 58.

"The sooner you begin, the sooner we can get back. You know darn well what your chores are on Saturdays. Hooper Ellen Hill, get your narrow behind down here now," Dorothy shouted!

"K, Mama Dot," Hoop replied.

"Say the whole word Hoop. Say it slowly o...k...a...y.," Dorothy instructed.

Dorothy then focused her attention elsewhere, her longtime

companion James Lewis. Their day had been previously planned and she wondered what had been taking him so long.

"He knows we have to make several stops today. And Lord knows I don't want to fuss with the Saturday crowd at Walmart," Dorothy complained.

"We going mart today, Mama Dot," Hoop asked?

"How many times do I have to tell you to stay out of grown folk business? Just stay near me and dust the coffee table in the living room until your breakfast is ready," a befuddled Dorothy declared.

Hoop's physique is still intact just as it was when she played her last game as a Lady Wolf at Cheyney High School. Although Hoop attends speech, physical therapy and counseling sessions regularly, she hasn't touched a basketball since that day. Dorothy attends group and individual counseling sessions as well.

The home is filled with promise and love. Hoop's awards, trophies, photographs and news articles are proudly displayed on the living room mantle. Everyone at school loved Hoop. Not just because she was the school's basketball star; but because of her warm heart, humor and spirit.

That's why they still come to visit. Her former coaches, teammates, classmates, you name it. They do most of the talking because Hoop's speech, neurological and behavioral patterns are not as they were. And every once and a while, she's able to complete full sentences and even have a full conversation. You just never know.

However, her biggest compulsion is to randomly shout out basketball trivia. Today, Hoop nearly completed a full sentence and Dorothy failed to notice.

"Goddammit! I forgot we have to take Mama's commode out

of your room and down to the junkyard. Then, I've got to pick up some meat from Pig Town[11]," Dorothy exclaimed!

Hoop casually picked up a bottle of nail polish remover and the dust rag that had been left on the coffee table and began to dust.

Sensing something was awry, Dorothy asked Hoop what she was doing.

A naked Hoop calmly replied, "Dusting Dot!"

"What! You better **put a handle on it** and watch how you speak to me! You might be 20 years old; but you better remember that I am still your mother! Put your night clothes back on your naked ass, Hoop! James will be here any minute! Now... I said," Dorothy shouted!

Hoop put her night clothes back on; a blue and white pair of shorts and a matching jersey- her Cheyney High School Basketball uniform. Minutes later, Mr. James walked in. He is a retired, car salesman and widower. He invested his money well after winning a large amount from the lottery. He wears loud cologne; but most importantly, he loves the ground that Dorothy walks on.

"Now before you start... I stopped at the **fillin station** and you won't believe who I saw sitting on the steps over on Mosher Street," James asked?

"James, I could care less about them negroes from the old neighborhood," Dorothy replied.

"I hate when you talk like that Dot. That's what's wrong with some of ya'll folks who move out to the county," James replied.

"And what's that," Dorothy asked?

"Ya'll forget where you came from! When I met you, you were a narrow little chocolate drop. And you played hopscotch with

---

[11] a neighborhood in the southern area of Baltimore. The area acquired its name during the second half of the 19th century, when the area was the site of butcher shops and meat packing plants to process pigs transported on the B&O Railroad.

your friends in the middle of Argyle Avenue. Did you forget," James asked?

"James, I know where I came from and I don't need you or nobody else to remind me. I lived it. I was there during the M.L.K riots. I know how hard my parents tried to save up and move us out of the old neighborhood. They tried their best. And my daddy died tryin. Mama did what she could to move me, Gerald and Jilly out of West Baltimore; but I'm glad that I saved up and moved on when I did. At my age, I don't know how I would have survived with all the changes, had I stayed. And I damn sure don't know what I would have done, had I seen another riot out there in the same streets some forty plus years later up close! It was bad enough to watch it on T.V.! I know where I came from and it aint't such a pretty story," Dorothy declared!

"Okay. Dorothy baby. I didn't mean to get you all worked up. Just guess who I saw," James asked again?

"Mitchell Hayes! Ha! He's a deacon now, over at First Christ Baptist. His wife Judith is still singing," James said.

Dorothy slammed James' plate on the kitchen table. Hoop moved slowly toward the back door. She stood there quietly and gazed out of the backdoor window.

"James, I've **got too many irons in the fire.** I don't have time to listen to you running your mouth about people who've already got **one foot in the grave**," Dorothy shouted!

"Dot, **God don't like ugly**," James said.

"What you talking about James? I check on them every now and then. I'm a busy person! And I am not gonna be a regular at wakes and funerals like your old girlfriend Urseline," Dorothy shouted!

"What you worrying about Urseline for? She **can't hold a candle to you**," James said.

Dorothy and James were completely engrossed in their conversation.

"She never did and never will. And don't you forget it! That old barfly likes to dig her claws into men, keep em drunk then wipe out their pensions," Dorothy, declared!

"What time would like to leave today darling," James smoothly asked?

"As soon as. Where is Hoop," Dorothy asked?

Dorothy ran to the kitchen window. She smiled to herself, as she watched Hoop standing quietly and naked in the backyard, gently running her fingers over the yellow mums they planted a week ago.

"Lawd! That gal is in the backyard butt- ass naked. I'll go get her," James said.

"Dammit...dammit..Going to Walmart...dammit.," Hoop said.

"Stop all that cussing Hoop and get your tail in the house," James shouted!

"When you catch her, wrap her in one of the sheets hanging on the clothesline!" Dorothy yelled from the kitchen window.

After James had completed three laps around Dorothy's cookie-cutter house, he realized an audience had formed. Assembled was the neighbor's 12 year old son, an elderly woman sitting on her porch, and the new mailman delivering mail across the street.

He said to himself, "Lawd, please help me. Cuz this child is crazy. Sometimes she acts just like her father. Down there in Georgia, with his old nasty self, chasing women and being a public nuisance."

"Come on girl. I'm too old for all this running," James shouted!

"No! Asshole! Ass! Asshole," Hoop shouted!

"I ain't gonna be too many more assholes, Hoop. Get in the house," James shouted!

Hoop ran from the clothesline and the planted mums in the backyard, past the viburnum and weigela bushes on the side of the house, before she slowed down and suddenly stopped at the Oak tree in the front yard.

"Need some help James," a familiar voice asked?

"Yes," James pleaded!

It was Rose Nowak, Dorothy's neighbor. The two moved on Benson Avenue the same year and have been good friends ever since. Rose's family migrated from Austria to the United States after World War ll.

She and Dorothy love planting flowers and vegetables together. Since Hoop's drastic change four years ago, Rose has become more like an auntie to Hoop than a neighbor.

"She's at it again huh," Rose asked?

Hoop smiled at Rose as she walked over and gave her a huge hug.

James took advantage of the calming moment and gently covered Hoop with the sheet that was still wrapped around his hands.

"D zien dobry[12] Hooper. I have something for you. Here taste it," Rose said.

"Apple?" Hoop asked as she sat under the Oak tree.

"No sweetheart it's a tomato," Rose said.

"It good," Hoop said.

"Thank you Hoop. I picked it this morning from my garden. It's nice and ripe. Say r.i p. e," Rose pronounced slowly.

"R.i i.," Hoop repeated.

James wiped his brow and sat under the tree next to Hoop. Dorothy walked down her front porch steps and joined everyone.

"Hey Rose! Did you know that Hoop could run faster than **pat and turner**," James asked?

"Are they new neighbors," Rose asked?

"Don't pay him no mind Rose," Dorothy said.

"No Rose. What I'm saying is Hoop can still run and move

---

[12] Polish for good morning.

quicker than you can pat your feet on the ground and turn the corner. It's an old saying. Ya'll didn't say that over there in Poland," James asked?

James glanced at Hoop, who was still nibbling on the tomato and said, "You know Hoop you can still be the next Tamecka Dixon. Yes indeedy," he said.

"Dorothy, I brought these for you. Sit them in the kitchen windowsill for now until they're ripe," Rose said.

"Rose, if you keep this up, the Sprouts Farmers Market, Giant and Wegmans markets will be coming to you to distribute their produce," Dorothy teased.

"I've got to go. On grandma duty today! See you later alligator," Rose teased.

"What you know about that Rose? After while crocodile," James replied.

"I'll pick up some kielbasa for you from Pig Town so you can make your Bigos stew later," Dorothy said.

"Do widzenia[13]," Rose said.

"Yeah, do Wednesday to you too, Rose! You ready, Dot," James asked?

"I want to stop at the mall first because next week I want me and Hoop to be put together real nice," Dorothy said.

"I still can't believe it. How's Jillian holding up," James asked?

"I can't call it James. I haven't spoken to her. You know how stubborn she is," Dorothy said.

"What's important is that we show support and pay our respect. And what I don't want, is you worrying about uppity folks. She's your sister. And we are family. Goddammit," James shouted!

---

[13] Polish for goodbye.

HOOP'S TRUTH

*Truth is--- She ain't my real mama. Her son died in a car accident when he was seven years old. Donald couldn't find steady work after he was let go from the steel company. His depression and drinking got worse. He drank morning, noon and night. He started putting hands on Dorothy. After 15 years of abuse she packed her bags and left. They've been separated for years. No one knows where he lives. However, people say every now and then they see Mr. Donald standing outside the bars begging for money and food. That's why she don't want to hear shiiit about the old neighborhood. Those days and people represent pain. She appreciates and loves Mr. James. He's **been sweet on her** since high school.*

And guess what? I've got a crush on the new mailman. That's why I ran out the house naked. Shucks, I know I look good!

GLORIA LYNN HOWE

*Tyrone Curtis "Muggsy" Bogues is known as the "shortest NBA player. He played point guard for four teams; the Charlotte Hornets, Washington Bullets, Golden State Warriors and the Toronto Raptors.

He developed his basketball skills in his hometown- Baltimore, Maryland. He attended the legendary Paul Laurence Dunbar High School where he famously played in 1982-1983.

Today, Bogues and his daughter Brittney run "Always Believe Incorporated," a non-profit organization that supports underprivileged middle and high school students in Charlotte, North Carolina.

10

Sisterly

Los Angeles / Keisha and Jillian

Keisha and Jillian sat in separate chairs in Keisha's living room, while Jayden, Keisha's youngest son, prepared a snack in the kitchen.

"Why are you looking out of the window? Nobody's gonna steal your ride. And as long as you didn't park along the red curb, you're straight. You're good," Keisha said.

"I'm not worried about that. This part of Gardena is nice," Jillian replied.

"I can't believe how tall Jayden's gotten. Is he still," Jillian said.

"He sure is playing basketball. He just made junior varsity," Keisha said.

"Look at us. Still reading each other's minds and completing each other's sentences. Where's James and Justin," Jillian asked?

"They're at their dads' this weekend. It's just me and my baby boy 'til Sunday. What brings you to my **neck of the woods**," Keisha asked?

"First, I'd like to thank you for having me on such short notice," Jillian said.

"Jill, you know you are always welcomed here. You sounded stressed over the phone. Is everything okay," Keisha asked?

"Yes. Well, uh," Jillian hesitated.

"For real what's up? And oh! Congratulations on the new job," Keisha said.

"That's why I'm here," Jillian said.

"Really," Keisha asked?

Keisha instructed Jayden to take his snack into his bedroom.

Jillian turned toward Keisha and looked her square in her eyes then cleared her throat.

Did you tell someone that I offered sexual favors to a few board members of the Ladera Heights Jack and Jill Chapter," she asked?

"What? Are you kidding," Keisha asked?

"Keisha! I worked my ass off. I didn't give it away," Jillian said.

Both Keisha and Jillian stood up and squared off face to face.

"Wait a minute Jillian! You ain't gonna come in my house starting some high school bullshit! And the way you are running off at the mouth, it sounds like you believe this crap," Keisha shouted!

"There's more. Did you say that I created a fake resume," she asked?

"You about to get your ass beat and put out! And to say this to me with my youngest in the other room! Where is all this coming from," Keisha asked?

"Someone heard you say it at our sorority affair," Jillian said.

"You have lost your mind! Are you going through the change? You need a prescription? I've got some black cohosh for your bougie high yella ass! Now tell me who heard me say that? Who? Who? You gonna come in here and ask me some dumb shit like this. Who said it Jill," Keisha asked?

Keisha and Jillian continued their face to face argument in the living room. They breathed heavily through their nostrils while their arms flailed at their sides. Until they heard Jayden call out.

"Mommy! Are you okay," Jayden asked?

"Yes, baby, Mommy and Auntie Jill are just talking loudly. See what you did heifer," Keisha responded through her teeth.

"Soror Jones told me," Jillian shouted!

"Gurl bye," Keisha said.

Keisha waved her hand in Jillian's face before sitting back down on the couch.

"What do you mean," Jillian asked?

"Girl, you never could **see the forest for the trees.** Soror Jones is a hot assed mess! Ever since the state snatched her administrative license with the California Unified School District, she's been on the warpath with anyone on their "**come up**." She is menopausal, bitter, jealous and plain ole mean. You can't believe a word that comes out of her mouth. Damn. Wait a minute," Keisha said.

"Keisha, I don't have anything to do with the school system. Other than the chapter we don't have a connection," Jillian said.

"Sit down donkey of the day. The connection is her husband, Dr. Edward Jones. He is a Jack and Jill Board Member." Keisha said.

"Wow," Jillian said.

"Wow is right! Now don't you owe me something? With your ole bougie and emotional self," Keisha said.

"I sure do. I'm sorry, Keesh. I didn't want to believe it," Jillian said.

"Jill do you remember that poem you wrote in high school called Girls Can't Be Friends? I used to believe every word in that poem. That poem reminds me of the old me. I was angry and envious of the girls who I thought were prettier than me and girls with lighter complexions. I spoke to my therapist about it. She said it stems from having colorism issues," Keisha admitted.

"Really, I can't believe you remember that poem," Jillian replied.

"Back then, we both were hurting. I don't believe those toxic words anymore. That may be the cause of Soror Jones' anger. It may also be the reason why you believed her. Not everyone is meant to stay in our lives forever. Some people we have to let go and some will leave on their own. You and I are more than just friends, we're family," Keisha said.

"Please forgive me, Keisha. I'll never doubt you again. And I'm sorry about everything I've said about you. On my mother's grave and on the shield," Jillian said.

"You don't have to go there, Jill. I still love you. Let's keep Soror Jones in prayer; but I'm going to keep a close eye on her old, gossiping, shady, dusty self. As for you, try not to wear those tight, form- fitted dresses around her man at work. Okay," Keisha joked.

"Girls Can't Be Friends"
By: Jillian Chanel Hill

Maplewood High School
Mrs. Sanders English Class
1st Period
Monday, May 22, 1981

She will love, but will never **encourage** you to reach your **dreams**. She will love you, go shopping with you, pray with you and hate everything about you– even down to your hair follicle. She will love you. She'll want to be you. And be with your boyfriend too!

She will love you and then tell your darkest and most sacred secrets to your enemies. She we love you when you are sick and bring you candy, cards and balloons, only to **be the first** to tell others how bad you look. She will love you until you can no longer love or _**trust in love**_ again.

The End!

GLORIA LYNN HOWE

HOOP'S TRUTH

Truth is-- Jillian has always been jealous of Keisha. Jillian's mother died when she was young. Her father had already passed. Her older sister was married; but her living arrangements were unstable. Her older brother lived in Georgia. His wife had recently given birth. It was rumored that she was suffering from postpartum depression. Therefore, she was sent to live with her elderly aunt and uncle in Los Angeles. She met Keisha and Bradley during their freshman year in high school. Keisha came from a large, close-knit family. Daniel, Keisha's first baby daddy was the high school's football star. Back then, Daniel only had eyes for Keisha. And little did everyone know that Jillian only had eyes for him.

*Elena Delle Donne left the University of Connecticut after two days and gave up basketball for a year to spend time with her older sister, Lizzie, who has cerebral palsy, is blind, deaf and has autism.

"Everyone thought I came home to help her; but she was the one helping me...." Donne currently plays for the Washington Mystics.

Delle Donne normally cares for her sister during the WNBA off season.

11

I Can't Cry Like I Want To

Topanga Canyon, Southern California

Nothing seemed to work. Not therapy, the discussions, the encouragement from family and friends– nor prayers. Bradley's **well was running dry**. That evening he decided to drive through Topanga Canyon from the San Fernando Valley. He hoped the scenic route, which lead to the slapping waves of Malibu Beach would help him to make a decision.

When Bradley reached a height of 1, 084 feet his cellphone rang. It was his dad. Bradley listened as his dad asked questions and gave more marital advice.

"Since she won't go, I'll go," he said. He navigated his way up and down, twisting and turning through the narrow and breathtaking canyon road.

"I've been doing the work dad. Yes, I'm taking my meds. I'm tired of trying to figure things out. And I'm tired of everyone's meddling.

Don't you get it! I'm who she needed not who she wanted! I've known since high school. She never wanted to marry me! Calm down? I am as calm as I can be given the circumstances. I'm headed to the beach to clear my head. Listen, I've made my decision. I've got a call coming in. I love you too dad," Bradley said

Bradley hung up and answered the other call.

"Bradley Logan speaking," he said.

"This is Joel Silva from Mountain Securities returning your call,"

Mr. Silva said.

"Yes, Mr. Silva I wanted to thank for forwarding the copies of the notaries. Everything looks great. Are you sure that everything's locked in? Thanks again," Bradley said.

Further down the canyon, Bradley parked at a landing near the edge of a cliff. It was less than a mile away from Malibu Beach. It was a familiar area. He and Jillian would sit there as teenagers in his father's sturdy Subaru under the moonlight and stars. There, they dreamt about their future as husband and wife. They nicknamed the area, "Our Little Piece of Heaven."

This time he stopped there for a different reason. He wanted to double check a few personal documents that were also included in the packet that Mr. Silva had notarized. The documents were letters that he'd written to his family.

To My Love Jillian

I love you. You are my heartbeat. Jilly I'm not at peace. I can't cry like I want to.

Our marriage and family were built on sinking sand. You've tried to save me; but I can't let my depression drown you and the kids any further.

To my Children,
James, you can make it to the NBA dude. Get some pointers from your Cousin Hoop. Baby boy, stolz auf dich[14]. John, take lots of pictures on your class trip to Munich. And to my dearest Jasmine, know that I am with you. If you stumble, make it a part of your dance before the Lord.
   "Peace I leave with you; my peace I give you..." John 14:27

---

[14] German for I'm proud of you

Just then, Bradley received another call. It was Angela Colon.

"Hello Angela. Sorry I didn't return your calls," Bradley said.

"I'm just checking on you, Bradley. How did the conversation go with Jillian," Angela asked?

Bradley started his car and made a turn.

"Uh, I'm in on my way to …..What the…," Bradley shouted!

"Bradley! Bradley! Bradley," Angela shouted!

HOOP'S TRUTH

Truth is— Bradley *was recently diagnosed with Stage 4 Prostate Cancer. For weeks, Angela has pleaded with him to share his diagnosis with his family. She threatened to tell Jillian herself after learning that he had refused chemotherapy treatment. He has reached his **fork in the road** both literally and figuratively.*

12

I've Got Your Back

Malibu / Jillian Logan & Sara Bergher

A stoic and disheveled Jillian sat alone in the waiting area of the UCLA Health Center in Malibu.

A doctor and nurse approached her.

"Mrs. Logan. We're sorry. He didn't make it," the doctor said.

"He...wha,"Jillian uttered.

"Is there anyone with you? Can we call someone for you," the nurse asked?

Jillian was speechless. She sat still and looked on. Other medical staffers gathered and readied themselves in preparation for a sudden breakdown.

"We tried everything; but he was unresponsive upon arrival. Who should we call Mrs. Logan," the doctor asked?

While the medical staff continued to soothe and question Jillian, another nurse, gently pried Jillian's purse from her hands.

"Where did they find him," Jillian asked?

"You'd have to speak to one of the gentlemen over there," a nurse said.

The man approached Jillian, the doctor and team of nurses.

"Mrs. Logan," I'm Captain Evans with the Malibu Search and Rescue Unit," he said.

"What happened," Jillian asked?

The staff placed Jillian on a gurney. Captain Evans continued to share information with Jillian as the staff wheeled her down several corridors and into a room.

"We received a call this afternoon around 3 p.m. stating that a car had run off a cliff on Topanga Canyon," Captain Evans said.

"Topanga Canyon," Jillian asked?

"Mrs. Logan is there anyone who may have wanted to harm your husband," Captain Evans asked?

"No! Everyone loved Bradley," Jillian said.

"With all due respect, is there any possibility that your husband would want to harm himself," Captain Evans asked?

Just then, Sara Bergher entered the room. The nurse who had possession of Jillian's purse and cellphone contacted her.

"She's not answering anymore questions. Can't you see she's in shock," Sara shouted!

"Sara! How did you," Jillian asked?

"I came as soon as I heard. Sweetheart I'm so sorry," she said.

"Mrs. Logan, you have our deepest sympathy. We thought you might want to read this before we turn it over to the police for their investigation. It's a letter we found in your husband's car," Captain Evans said.

"To My love, Jillian. He was there? We called it "Our Little Piece of Heaven." Why, Sara? Why," Jillian asked?

Then Jillian released. She let out the loudest scream ever. Then she cried and cried and cried. Her tears were endless. She tossed and turned all night. The nurses eventually strapped her to the bed. Sara stayed with her until she fell asleep.

The next morning, Jillian called her sister Dorothy in Maryland from her hospital room.

"He's gone Dot," Jillian said.

"Who's gone," Dorothy asked?

"Brad," Jillian said.

"Gone where? Talk to me straight Jill," Dorothy demanded!

"He's with Mommy and Daddy in heaven now," Jillian said.

After Jillian explained as much as she could to her sister Dot, she called her sorority sister, Reesa in New York. The two were line sisters and are still **as thick as thieves**.

"No Jill," Reesa shouted!

"I need you Reesa," Jillian said.

"I'm on my way, Sands.[15] I've got your back," Reesa said.

---

[15] A Greek sorority and fraternity pledge sister or brother.

HOOP'S TRUTH

Truth is-- Jillian is Dorothy Hill's younger sister. I loved Uncle Brad. Everyone loved him. Uncle Brad seemed to be the only one who really understood my disorder. He never stopped bragging about my basketball skills. I planned to show him how much my social skills and speech had improved this summer. He was special to me. And although it seems like my Aunt Jillian does not know how to be a good wife, sister or friend, she can be. There's just something deep inside that has been troubling her soul since she was a little girl. And the only person who seems to know her best is her Line Sister Reesa. She brings out the good in Jillian. This funeral should be interesting.

13

Hold Your Peace

Family, friends and colleagues all gathered to celebrate the life of Bradley Logan at the Church of Holiness in Ladera Heights. The church was packed. People from all walks of life were there. It was a testament to his life and it spoke volumes of how much he was loved and respected.

Sara entered the church office. Jillian and Jasmine were there waiting for the service to begin.

"Sara, you shouldn't have," Jillian said.

"Bradley was a member of our family too. Besides, you were in no condition to make the arrangements. I'll see you out there shortly." Sara said.

The two hugged. Sara exited the church office as Angela walked in.

"Ooh Mommy look. There are a lot of people in the church," Jasmine said.

"Move away from the door. No one is to see you yet," Jillian said.

"Why? I want to look at the people," Jasmine whined.

"This is why I didn't want her to be here! She's almost the

same age that I was when my mother my mother. Where are your brothers," Jillian asked?

"Don't worry. Children are resilient, Jill. You two stay put. I'll go look for them," Angela said.

Angela left to find James and John.

Reesa and Jeffrey flew in from New York the night before. The two are seated on a church pew.

"Thank you for coming with me, Jeffrey," Reesa said.

"And miss out on a free trip to L.A? Besides, who else can help you keep your face beat while you cry," Jeffrey said.

"I haven't cried since the Debra Moore incident at the salon," Reesa joked.

"Chil, you should have won an academy award for that performance! It was genius of you to cry with her over her husband. Not once did you ever mention his name. Before I knew it, the two of you were giving each other advice on how to move on from the same damn man," Jeffrey said!

"God is good Jeffrey," Reesa said.

"All the time. And it's good that you're here with Jillian too. I know you are out here in support of your Soror; but truth is you needed the time away. I'll hold things down at the Salon. Take your time coming back. Your staff and I love you Reesa," Jeffrey said.

Seated on another pew were Keisha and Abeba.

"The parking was crazy. Thanks for holding a seat for me, Keesh," Abeba said.

"Yes, it's a full house. I still can't believe it, Abeba. Jill and I just made plans for Brad and our boys to play basketball in a few weeks," Keisha said.

"We've got to keep her close. Has her family arrived from Maryland yet," Abeba asked?

"Yes. And Reesa flew in from New York," Keisha said.

"Oh, good. Keesha is that the pastor," Abeba asked?

"Yup, that's Pastor Harris. I heard he can preach. I have no doubt that he'll **set the house on fire** today," Keisha said.

"He's setting me on fire now. Look how his rope sways when he walks," Abeba said.

"You nasty Abeba," Keisha snapped.

Angela found James and John laughing and goofing off with a relative in the church parking lot. The three headed back toward the church. Malcolm had just parked his car. He caught up with Angela and the boys as they headed back inside the church.

"Thanks for letting me drive us here. Bradley was my friend, too," Malcolm said.

"I know you were. Why don't you find seats for us? I want to bring the boys in to Jillian and speak with them in private. I'll join you before the service begins," she said.

"Okay, I love you, Angela," he said.

"I love you too. And Malcolm, the answer is yes," Angela said.

Inside the church office.

"Where have you two been," Jillian asked?

"We were in the parking lot listening to Uncle Gerald's wild and crazy stories," John said.

"James, John and you too, Jasmine. Uncle Gerald is a nut! I want you to stay the hell away from him! Lord, give me strength," Jillian screamed!

"Jillian, there's something you and the kids should know," Angela said.

"Tell us later, Angela," Jillian said.

"No! Now is the time. It may help you understand," Angela said.

"What I understand is that my husband is dead! I still don't know whether this was by his own doing or if it was an accident.

What I do know is that he is lying in a coffin, Angela," Jillian shouted!

"He had cancer," Angela shouted!

"Cancer," Jillian shouted!

"He confided in me several months ago. I referred him to an oncologist, but he refused treatment. I've been pleading with him to tell you," she said.

"How could I have been so blind," Jillian asked?

The Eulogy

"The word says…… in John 3:16 that "For God so loved the world that he gave his only begotten Son….," Pastor Harris said.

From a front pew.

"For God so, so, so loved this world, that he took Bradley straight on up to heaven. Hallelujah," Gerald yelled and somewhat sang.

"Ain't nobody asked him to sing. James, please take Gerald out of here," Dorothy pleaded.

"Honey who is that carrying on like that," Bradley Logan Sr. asked?

"I don't know sweetheart. It must be one of Jillian's relatives," Mrs. Logan said.

Others in the church were distracted. While some seemed entertained by Gerald's vocal rendition, Pastor Harris was unmoved.

"Amen brother. Church, we are gathered here today to celebrate the life of a good man…," Pastor Harris said.

Dorothy nudged James with her elbow so he could shut Gerald up or take him out of the church. James angrily turned to face to Gerald.

"Look here man this ain't the place. Gerald, you can't be

hoopin and hollerin like this. Why don't you cool off outside," James asked?

"Hold up, James! I didn't finish sanging my song. I gotta a right to be here too," Gerald declared!

"How the hell are you here anyway? Wasn't you in jail," James asked?

"You know they can't keep a good man down. The Good Lord made it so for them gals to drop the charges," Gerald replied.

"Well, sit on the other side next to your daughter and **hold your peace**," James demanded!

Gerald begrudgingly agreed and sat quietly at the end of the pew next to Hoop.

"Peace I leave with you... For I do not give to you the peace of this world…; but let not your hearts be troubled… brothers and sisters….," Pastor Harris said.

"Shit," Hoop shouted!

"Be quiet, Hoop," a startled Dorothy said.

"Stop this shit," Hoop shouted again!

Dorothy nudged Hoop with her elbow several times; but that only made Hoop talk louder. Amazingly, Gerald sat back quietly and grinned.

"Keep her quiet, Dot! I'm sorry, Pastor, she doesn't know what she's saying," Jillian said.

"I'm doing the best I can Jill. Shhh, Hoop. I know this might be hard for you baby; but please try to show some respect," Dorothy pleaded.

"She needs to get her shit together! Aunt Jillian, stop worrying about what people think. Your nose has been up people's asses so much that you've never been able to think straight. You couldn't even see how much your husband was hurting. His hurt literally drove him to his death. Change, Jillian! Do it for your children, for your sister and for my daddy," Hoop shouted!

"Out of the mouth of babes. Let the church say Amen," Pastor Harris shouted!

"Hallelujah! That's right baby. Speak the truth baby," Bradlely's mother shouted!"

During the repast in the church basement.

"Lord I thank you. I'm so proud of you Hoop. Your words were so beautiful. Keep talking baby," Dorothy said.

"You're Jillian's sister. Nice to finally meet you. I'm Sara Bergher and this is my husband Erick. Bradley spoke so highly of you, Sara said.

"Aww. Nice to meet you too," Dorothy said.

"And she must be the family's basketball star, Ms. Hooper Hill," Sara said.

"Yes, she is," Dorothy said.

"If you'd like, I can get floor seats at the Staples Center. The Lakers play tomorrow night," Sara said.

"Now **that's what the doctor ordered**," James said.

"And this is my one and only, Mr. James Lewis. James this is Mr. and Mrs. Bergher," Dorothy said.

"Glad to meet you. I'll leave the tickets at the will call. And please let us know if you need anything. Really anything," Sara said.

"Thank you so much. We really appreciate your generosity," Dorothy said.

"Hey, Hoop! There's a basketball court in the community room. Let's go," John said.

"Well, what about your sister and brother James," Dorothy asked?

"Aunt Dot, they're spying for us now. Pastor Harris and a few deacons challenged us to play a game. Now that we've got Hoop as our coach, Uncle Gerald, Mr. Malcolm and myself on a team, I know we'll crush em," John yelled!

HOOP

"And that was the truth. The score was 28-10! I love my family. We all have flaws; but essentially our hearts are good. Being different, odd and sometimes misunderstood can be difficult; but somehow we manage. As you've seen everyone was different in their own beautiful and special way,"
Hooper Ellen Hill

About the Author

Gloria Lynn Howe

*Born in Baltimore, Maryland, Ms. Howe is best known for her first book, "**And Mother Used to Say..Words to Live By that "Ain't never Lied**," a compilation of common sense language and words of wisdom spoken by grandmothers and aunties from generations of old. Ms. Howe is an alumna of Cheyney University of Pennsylvania, the nation's oldest HBCU. She received a Master's degree at Mercy College in Dobbs Ferry, New York in secondary education specializing in English Language Arts. She is a former educator and print journalist. Ms. Howe is also a proud and active member of Delta Sigma Theta Sorority Incorporated. For bookings visit, www.Gloria Howe.com., or follow social media content on Instagram and Twitter @Gloria Howe and on Facebook at Gloria Lynn Howe #And Mother Used To Say.*

Acknowledgements & Special Comments

To God Be the Glory! *With a humble heart I give all praises and honor to my heavenly father. Thank you for your grace, mercy and favor. Thank you for keeping and blessing me time and time again.*

*Thank you **Shirley R. Bolding** for believing in me. You've been my rock, confidant, advisor and friend. Your love is undeniable. You are a blessing to many. In my opinion, you have already earned your wings.*

On the outside we may appear to be total opposites; but we are sisters in many ways. When I was younger, I truly believed that you and your friends had become nurses. It was your high school graduation day and you all wore white dresses. That story always makes me laugh because years later, I also wore white as I graduated from Western High School. Just as the color white symbolizes purity, it also represents the pureness of your heart. You've modeled "quiet dignity" long before I learned what it really meant.

I couldn't have made it through this journey or the other journeys in my life without you. I love you dear Cousin-Sister.

*And to my **Cousin Hooper Ellis Johnson**, thank you for your love and support. You are a survivor and a blessing to us all!*

I love you Cuzzos!

*Thank you to **Reverend Marcus G. Wood & Reverend Dr. Douglass E. Summers, Co- Pastors and the congregation of Providence Baptist Church** located in Baltimore, Maryland for your continued prayers, encouragement, love and fellowship.*

*Many thanks to my dearest friend, the one and only, **Actress, BeBe Drake**, I will always remember the day that we became friends. We were on a movie set in Virginia and you and I were casted as mother and daughter.*

At that time, I was grieving the loss of my mother Shirley Chambers. I shared with you and you lifted my spirits.

Over the years we became family. Thank you for your advice, encouragement and memories. You are full of life, love and invaluable wisdom. Thank you for supporting my book from the beginning. Please give your granddaughter, B an extra hug & kiss for me. When it comes to seeing this book seen on the big or small screen- I am faithful. As the saying goes, from our lips to God's ears.

*To my dear friend **Actor, Reno Wilson**, from our early years in Los Angeles to the present, you've remained the same. You are an **"incredible actor."** What I've known since day one is that you are a beautiful, generous and sincere person.*

Thank you for our continued friendship, laughter and the gift that you share with the world. Most importantly, thank you for believing in my book from the beginning. I wish you and your beautiful family continued blessings.

*Thank you to my dear friend, **Author, writer and producer, Doreen Spicer-Dannelly**, muchas gracias senorita! Thank you for our talks, texts and everything in between. In my Heavy D voice, I've got nothing; but Brooklyn, California, books and HBCU Love 4 Ya Baby! You are a light and an inspiration!*

*Many thanks to **Ms. Ameerah Holliday** for your crisp editorial reviews. Keep sending your creative and inspirational vibes out through poetry. Much success to **Ebb & Flow Publications.***

In Memoriam:

*Thank you **Allegra Bennett, Author**, of **"<u>Renovating Woman</u>"**, and former journalist for the Baltimore Sun and the Washington Times. I always wondered where you worked. After I learned what a journalist did and that one lived across the street from me, I was in awe. I became that pesky neighbor; who was really just a little girl who wanted to grow up and write for a living too. Back then, I wasn't totally invested and you knew it;*

but you tolerated my queries day after day and year after year. When the time came, you took me under your wing and became my writing mentor.

You watched me mature as I grew professionally; from a writing fellow, editorial assistant, budding journalist to a full-time daily news reporter. Thank you for sharing your wit and wisdom. And thank you for being my friend and an encouraging light.

*Thank you **Dr. Joseph P. Rayapati, Professor of English at Cheyney University of Pennsylvania**. You believed in me before I believed in myself. Thank you for allowing me to spread my wings as a communication arts student. From freshman year on, you helped me to develop my writing, reporting and public speaking skills.*

You challenged me to write about unfamiliar subjects. That challenge led to my first bylined feature in a Pennsylvania magazine. Thank you for introducing me to Toastmasters International. And thank you for being an invested and firm educator. You will always be remembered.

To my family and friends both near and far, thank you, thank you and thank you!

I love you all,
Gloria

Book Club Discussion Questions & Connections

1. Did you relate to Hoop's story in any way? If so, how?
2. Which character did you like most?
3. Which chapter did you like most?
4. Were the characters relatable?
5. Have you or someone you know been affected by a topic(s) mentioned in the book?
6. Which character(s) would you like to learn more about?
7. Which chapter would you like to read as a full novel?
8. Which old-fashioned saying or idiom was familiar?
9. Which NBA and or WNBA player did you appreciate learning about?
10. What did you enjoy most about reading **"Hoop's Truth"-A Novella**?

Join the conversation @ www.gloriahowe.com

Hoop's Basketball Trivia

Mahmoud Abdul-Rauf, who played for the Denver Nuggets, Sacramento Kings and the Vancouver Grizzlies, had a mild version of "Tourette's syndrome," that went undiagnosed until he was 17. He said the syndrome encouraged him to seek perfection and obtain great results. He managed to overcome the difficulties and is considered one of the greatest free throw shooters in NBA history.

Born Chris Wayne Jackson, he is also known for refusing to stand for the national anthem during a game against the Chicago Bulls in Chicago. Instead of pledging his allegiance to the American flag, he demonstrated his protest by praying. In 1996, the NBA suspended him for the protest. During his suspension he lost millions. However, with the support of the players union, the NBA reached a quick compromise with the league that allowed him to return under the "stand and pray with their head down" agreement during the anthem. This policy allows players who practice diverse religions to honor their beliefs during the anthem. Although this NBA great lost millions, he remains unapologetic and says he has no regrets.

"I don't criticize those who stand, so don't criticize me for sitting," **Mahmoud Abdul-Rauf**

Hoop's Basketball Trivia

Sheryl Denise Swoopes is the first player to be signed in the WNBA. She is the first women's basketball player to have a Nike shoe named after her: The "Air Swoopes." She is currently the Assistant Coach for the Lady Raiders Women's Basketball Team at Texas Tech, her alma mater.

Cookie Johnson is not only the legendary "Magic Earvin Johnson's" devoted wife, she is also a philanthropist. She serves as Secretary of Directors for the Magic Johnson Foundation. The foundation focuses on health, social, and educational needs of underserved communities. For many years, Mrs. Johnson and her husband have advocated and fought for HIV/AIDS prevention and testing in underserved communities,

Hoop's Basketball Trivia

Although Lebron James gave everything he had in the 2018 NBA Finals with a 124-114 score in favor of the Golden State Warriors, he continued to be one of most influential and popular athletes in the NBA and off the court. He opened the "Promise School in Akron, Ohio on July 30, 2018. The charter school is partnered with The James Family Foundation and the Akron Public Schools.

However, most NBA fans famously remember that after failing to win a championship with the Cleveland Cavaliers, James' next move was wildly anticipated. He opted to become a free agent. And in 2010, he signed with the Miami Heat, a move that was titled, **"The Decision,"** It became one of the most controversial free agent decisions in American sports history.

Hoop's Basketball Trivia

Nancy Lieberman, nicknamed "Lady Magic," is a former professional basketball player and WNBA coach. The legendary basketball professional was born in Brooklyn, NY and served as Assistant Coach for the Sacramento Kings from 2015 to 2018. She is currently a broadcaster for the New Orleans Pelicans of the NBA.

To many Dennis Keith Rodman was one of the "greatest rebounders" ever. He played for the Detroit Pistons, San Antonio Spurs, Chicago Bulls, Los Angeles Lakers and the Dallas Mavericks. And because of infamous rebounding and defensive abilities, he was nicknamed, "The Worm."

Hoop's Basketball Trivia

Maya April Moore plays for the Minnesota Lynx. She played forward the University of Connecticut Women's Basketball Team from 2007-2011. The undefeated Huskies won two consecutive national championships in 2009 and 2010 and again in the 2010 and 2011 basketball season.

That same year, she led the UConn Huskies to break an NCAA gender record in all divisions of 90. Moore is the first female basketball player to sign with Air Jordan.

Nicknamed "The Hick from French Lick," **Larry Joe Bird** is widely regarded as one of the greatest basketball players of all time. From 1979 to 1992, he played for the Boston Celtics as both a small forward and power forward. He is credited as earning 21,791 points, 8,974 rebounds and 5,695 assists.

He was born in West Baden Springs, Indiana and attended Springs Valley High School in French Lick, Indiana, hence his nickname. After retiring from the NBA, he served as head coach of the Indian Pacers from 1997 to 2000. He currently serves as President of Basketball Operation for the Indiana Pacers.

"Hoop's Truth"- A Novella, is a smart and enticing contemporary story. Narrated by Hooper Ellen Hill, a six foot five teenaged basketball dreamer, who not only plays the game; but is obsessed with basketball trivia.

Although she has trouble socializing and communicating, Hoop is more observant than most. Through her, the lives of her colorful family and friends are revealed.

The relatable characters share their personal truths and a variety of difficulties with autism, depression, family, love and more in this interesting vignette.

Inspired by her first book, **"And Mother Used To Say...Words to Live By that "Ain't never Lied,"** Howe also blends clever clichés and old- fashioned idioms into the heart and soul of each passage. **"Hoop's Truth"- A Novella- an engaging experience!**

"This is a "CAN'T PUT DOWN BOOK!
You are there with the different characters and feeling their emotions.
"Hoop's Truth"- A Novella- I can't wait for the movie!"
BeBe Drake, Actress

"What a clever and witty way to merge the worlds of basketball and autism. It's funny and thoughtful. You'll want more!"
Reno Wilson, Actor